Oscar Fingal O'Flahertie Wills Wilde (16 October 1854 – 30 November 1900) was an Irish poet and playwright. After writing in different forms throughout the 1880s, he became one of London's most popular playwrights in the early 1890s. He is best remembered for his epigrams and plays, his novel The Picture of Dorian Gray, and the circumstances of his criminal conviction for homosexuality, imprisonment, and early death at age 46. Wilde's parents were successful Anglo-Irish intellectuals in Dublin. Their son became fluent in French and German early in life. At university, Wilde read Greats; he proved himself to be an outstanding classicist, first at Trinity College Dublin, then at Oxford. He became known for his involvement in the rising philosophy of aestheticism, led by two of his tutors, Walter Pater and John Ruskin. After university, Wilde moved to London into fashionable cultural and social circles. (Source: Wikipedia)

Literary works:
Ravenna (1878)
Poems (1881)
The Happy Prince and Other Stories (1888)
Lord Arthur Savile's Crime and Other Stories (1891)
A House of Pomegranates (1891)
Intentions (1891)
The Picture of Dorian Gray (1890)
The Soul of Man under Socialism (1891)
Lady Windermere's Fan (1892)
A Woman of No Importance (1893)
An Ideal Husband (1898)
The Importance of Being Earnest (1898)
De Profundis (1905)
The Ballad of Reading Gaol (1898)
The Portrait of Mr. W. H. (1889)

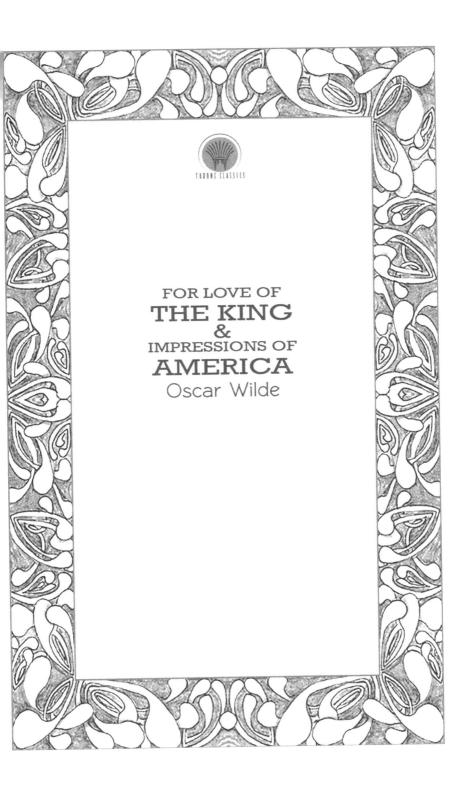

THRONE CLASSICS

FOR LOVE OF
THE KING
&
IMPRESSIONS OF
AMERICA
Oscar Wilde

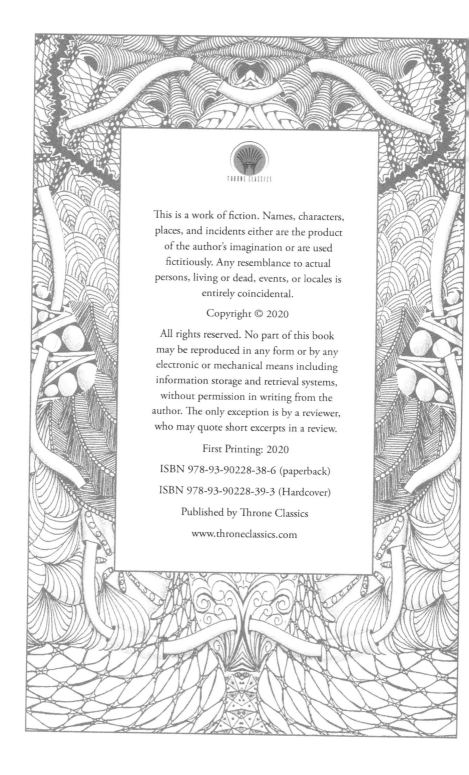

First Printing: 2020

ISBN 978-93-90228-38-6 (paperback)

ISBN 978-93-90228-39-3 (Hardcover)

Published by Throne Classics

www.throneclassics.com

Contents

FOR LOVE OF
THE KING
&
IMPRESSIONS OF
AMERICA

FOR LOVE OF THE KING

INTRODUCTORY NOTE

The very interesting and richly coloured masque or pantomimic play which is here printed in book form for the first time, was invented sometime in 1894 or possibly a little earlier. It was written, not for publication, but as a personal gift to the author's friend and friend of his family, Mrs. Chan Toon, and was sent to her with the letter that follows and explains its origin.

Mrs. Chan Toon, before her marriage to Mr. Chan Toon, a Burmese gentleman, nephew of the King of Burma and a barrister of the Middle Temple, was Miss Mabel Cosgrove, the daughter of Mr. Ernest Cosgrove of Lancaster Gate, a friend of Sir William and Lady Wilde, and herself brought up with Oscar and his brother Willie.

For a long while Mrs. Chan Toon, who after her husband's death became Mrs. Woodhouse-Pearse, refused to permit the masque to be printed. The late Robert Ross much wanted to include it in an edition of Wilde's works, of which it now forms a part, but he could not obtain its owner's consent. An arrangement, however, having been completed, the play is now made public.

Tite Street, Chelsea,

November 27, 1894

My dear Mrs. Chan Toon,

I am greatly repentant being so long in acknowledging receipt of "Told on the Pagoda." I enjoyed reading the stories, and much admired their quaint and delicate charm. Burmah calls to me.

Under another cover I am sending you a fairy play entitled "For Love of the King," just for your own amusement. It is the outcome of long and luminous talks with your distinguished husband in the Temple and on the river, in the days when I was meditating writing a novel as beautiful and as intricate as a Persian praying-rug. I hope that I have caught the atmosphere.

I should like to see it acted in your Garden House on some night when the sky is a sheet of violet and the stars like women's eyes. Alas, it is not likely.

I am in the throes of a new comedy. I met a perfectly wonderful person the other day who unconsciously has irradiated my present with sinuous suggestion: a Swedish Baron, French in manner, Athenian in mind, and Oriental in morals. His society is a series of revelations. . . .

I was at Oakley Street on Thursday; my mother tells me she sends you a letter nearly every week.

Constance desires to be warmly remembered, while I, who am bathing my brow in the perfume of water-lilies, lay myself at the feet of you and yours.

OSCAR WILDE

PRINCIPAL CHARACTERS OF THE PLAY

KING MENG BENG (*Lord of a Thousand White Elephants, Countless Umbrellas and other attributes of greatness*).

U. RAI GYAN THOO (*A Prime Minister*).

SHAH MAH PHRU (*A Girl, half Italian, half Burmese, of dazzling beauty*).

DHAMMATHAT (*Legal Adviser to the Court*).

HIP LOONG (*A Chinese Wizard of great repute*).

MOUNG PHO MHIN (*Minister of Finance*).

TWO ENVOYS FROM THE KING OF CEYLON.

NOBLES, COURTIERS, SOOTHSAYERS, POONYGEES, DANCING GIRLS, BETEL-NUT CARRIERS, UMBRELLA BEARERS, FOLLOWERS, SERVANTS, SLAVES, amongst whom are several CHINESE but no INDIANS.

TIME: *The Sixteenth Century.*

ACT I

SCENE I

The palace of the king of burmah. The scene is laid in the Hall of a Hundred Doors. In the distance can be seen the moat, the waiting elephants, and the peacocks promenading proudly in the blinding sunshine of late afternoon. The scene discovers king meng beng seated on a raised cushion sewn with rubies, under a canopy supported by four attendants, motionless as bronze figures. By his side is a betel-nut box, glittering with gems. On either side of him, but much lower down, are the two ambassadors of the king of ceylon, bearers of the King of Ceylon's consent to the marriage of his only daughter to Meng Beng in two years' time, men of grave, majestic mien, clad in flowing robes almost monastic in their white simplicity. They smoke gravely at the invitation of meng beng.

Round about are grouped the courtiers, the poonygees, and the kneeling servants, while in the background wait the dancing girls. Banners, propelled with a measured rhythm, create an agreeable breeze. On a great table of gold stand goblets of gold and heaped-up fruits. Everywhere will be observed the emblems of the Royal Peacock and the Sacred White Elephant. Burmese musical instruments sound an abrupt but charming discord. The poinsettias flower punctuates points of deepest colour from out of vases fashioned like the lotus. Orchids are everywhere. The indescribable scent of Burmah steals across the footlights. The glow, the colour, the sun-swept vista sweeps across the senses. the king claps his hands. The dancing girls, at the signal, advance. They are clad in dresses made of fish scales, which are fastened with diamonds and pale emeralds, to imitate the upthrown spray on the crest of a wave. The dance concluded, the cingalese ambassadors rise and prepare to take ceremonious leave of the king, who hands to them, through his vizier, his message to His Majesty of Ceylon, inscribed on palm leaves and enclosed in a bejewelled casket.

Many flowery speeches pass. Exit (L.), walking backwards.

the king expresses a desire for rest before starting by the Moon of Taboung [4] for the Pagoda of Golden Flowers.

Exit meng beng (C.), an alcove of satin hangings which commands a view of the great hall.

The Crowd break up into groups. u. rai gyan thoo and moung pho mhin converse on the tendency of the King to interference in affairs of State; his extreme youth and delicacy of temperament; the pity that the marriage is to be so long delayed; the necessity to find him some distraction in the meantime.

Suddenly the tom-toms sound loudly. There is much movement. The moon rises over the sea. Torches flare as the attendants move to and fro in the gardens beyond.

The White Elephant of the King, with its trappings of gold, is led to the entrance where, at a word, it sinks obediently to the ground.

the king appears. He has changed his gay apple-green dress to one of more sombre hue. He enters the howdah—the elephant rises—the procession starts. It consists of not fewer than two hundred persons, keeping in view of the audience until lost by a bend in the avenue.

SCENE II

THE PAGODA OF GOLDEN FLOWERS

Midnight

Surrounded by Peepul-trees, the great Htee, [6] with its crown of a myriad jewels, rises towards the violet, star-studded sky, its golden bells tinkling in a soft night-wind.

When the curtain rises, the circular platform is deserted. Statues of Buddha seated and recumbent fill the numberless niches in the wall, and before each burn long candles; heaped-up pink roses and japonica on brass

16

trays are lit from above by swinging coloured lamps. At intervals are stalls laden with fruit and cheroots. All is mysterious, solemn, beautiful.

A deep Burmese gong tolls. People emerge from the four staircases that lead up to the platform. Men, women, and children, all in gala attire. The young people conversing, gesticulating, smiling. The older people, more subdued, carry beads and votive offering to Buddha. Charming Burmese girls, with huge cigars, meet and greet handsome Burmese men smoking cheroots and wearing flowers in their ears. Children play silently with coloured balls. In the corners, under canopies, are seated fortune-tellers, busy casting horoscopes. It is a veritable riot of colour, with never a discordant note.

Through the crowd the king passes alone and unrecognised, and disappears through double doors of heavily carved teak wood. He has hardly passed when mah phru, a very lovely girl, enters in distress. She whispers that she desires an audience of the King who has come amongst them. The few who hear her shrug their shoulders, smile, and pass on. They are incredulous. She goes from group to group, but the people turn from her with disdain. Then the great doors open, and the king is seen. The girl throws herself, Oriental fashion, in his path. Her beauty and her pathos arrest his attention and he waves aside those who would interfere. She implores the king's protection. She is willing to be his slave. He listens with deep attention. She explains that since her father's death she has been continuously persecuted by the village people on the double count of her Italian blood and her poverty.

The girl invites him to come to her hut in the forest and verify what she says. With a gesture he signifies that he will follow where she leads. She rises. The crowd gathers round—all are hushed to silence. the king, as one entranced, puts aside all who would in any way interfere. The girl precedes him, going from the Pagoda towards the night. When she reaches the great staircase, she beckons, Oriental fashion, with downward hand. The scene should, in grouping and colour, make for rare beauty.

SCENE III

A humble dhunni-thatched hut, set amidst the whispering grandeur of the jungle, with its mighty trees, its trackless paths, its indescribable silence. The curtain discovers mah phru and the king, who expresses his amazement at the loneliness and the poverty of her lot. She explains that poverty is not what frightens her, but the enmity of those who live yonder, and who make it almost impossible for her to sell her cucumbers or her pineapples. the king's gaze never leaves the face or figure of the girl. He declares that he will protect her—that he will build her a home here in the shadow of the loneliness around them. He has two years of an unfettered freedom—for those years he can command his life. He loves her, he desires her—they will find a Paradise together. The girl trembles with joy—with fear—with surprise. "And after two years?" she asks. "Death," he answers.

ACT II

SCENE I

The jungle once more. Time: noonday. In place of the hut is a building, half Burmese, half Italian villa, of white Chunam, with curled roofs rising on roofs, gilded and adorned with spiral carvings and a myriad golden and jewel-encrusted bells. On the broad verandahs are thrown Eastern carpets, rugs, embroideries.

The world is sun-soaked. The surrounding trees stand sentinel-like in the burning light. Burmese servants squat motionless, smoking on the broad white steps that lead from the house to the garden. The crows croak drowsily at intervals. Parrots scream intermittently. The sound of a guitar playing a Venetian love-song can be heard coming from the interior. Otherwise life apparently sleeps. Two elderly retainers break the silence.

"When will the Thakin tire of this?" one asks the other in kindly contempt.

"The end is already at hand. I read it at dawn to-day."

"Whence will it come?"

"I know not. It is written that one heart will break."

"He will leave her?"

"He will leave her. He will have no choice—who can war with Fate?"

The sun shifts a little; a light breeze kisses the motionless palm leaves—they quiver gracefully. Attendants appear R. and L. bearing a great Shamiana (tent), silver poles, carved chairs, foot supports, fruit, flowers, embroidered fans. Three musicians in semi-Venetian-Burmese costume follow with their instruments. The tent erected, enter (C.) meng beng and mah phru, followed by two Burmese women carrying two tiny children in Burmese fashion on their hips.

The servants retire to a distance. meng beng and mah phru seat themselves on carven chairs; the children are placed at their feet and given coloured glass balls to play with. meng beng and mah phru gaze at them with deep affection and then at each other.

The musicians play light, zephyr-like airs. meng beng and mah phru talk together. meng beng smokes a cigar, mah phru has one of the big yellow cheroots affected by Burmese women to-day.

"It wants but two days to the two years," he tells her sadly.

"And you are happy?"

"As a god."

She smiles radiantly. She suspects nothing. She is more beautiful than before. Her dress is of the richest Mandalay silks. She wears big nadoungs of rubies in her ears.

Presently meng beng arranges a set of ivory chessmen on a low table between them. The sun sinks slowly. The sound of approaching wheels is heard.

Enter (C.) u. rai gyan thoo, preceded by two servants. meng beng looks up in surprise—in alarm. He rises, etc., and goes forward. u. rai gyan thoo presents a letter written on palm leaves. meng beng does not open it.

The curtains at the opening of the tent are, Oriental fashion, dropped. The music ceases.

meng beng and the grand vizier converse apart. The Minister explains that the Princess of Ceylon's ship and its great convoy have already been sighted. The Court and city wait in eager expectancy. The King has worshipped long enough at the Pagoda of Golden Flowers—his subjects and his bride call to him. u. rai gyan thoo has come to take him to them.

meng beng is terribly distressed.

"You can return one day," the Vizier tells him. "The Pagoda will remain. I also, once, in years long dead, Lord of the Sea and Moon, worshipped at a Pagoda."

meng beng seeks mah phru to explain that he goes on urgent affairs, that he will come back to her and to his sons, perhaps before the waning of the new moon. Their parting is sad with the pensive sadness of look and gesture peculiar to Eastern people.

meng beng goes (C.) with u. rai gyan thoo. mah phru mounts to the verandah to watch them go from behind the curtains. Then, slowly sinking across the heaped-up cushions, she faints.

The sun has set. The music ceases. The melancholy cry of the peacocks fills the silence.

ACT DROP

ACT III

SCENE I

Seven years have elapsed.

The same scene.

Curtain discovers mah phru seated on a high verandah. A clearance has been made in the surrounding trees to give a full view of the road beyond. She is watching, always watching. With her are two beautiful little boys.

"To-day, perhaps," she murmurs. "Perhaps to-morrow; but without fail—one day."

"Look!" she cries. "At last my lord returns!"

Coming up the jungle road, in view of the audience, are a bevy of horsemen.

mah phru, wondering, descends to greet them. Enter u. rai gyan thoo. He is dressed all in white, which is Burmese mourning. mah phru sinks back—she fears the worst. The old man reassures her. He tells her that meng beng has sent for his sons—that the Queen is dead, and there is no heir.

"Queen? What Queen?" demands mah phru.

"The Queen of Burmah."

So mah phru learns for the first time that her lover is the ruler of the country, supreme master of and dictator to everyone.

Weeping, but not daring to disobey, she summons the children to her; then, sinking on her knees, entreats in moving and pathetic words to be permitted to go with them, in the lowest most menial capacity. u. rai gyan thoo refuses. There is no place for her in the greatness of the world yonder.

"Even Kings forget," he says. "It is the command of the supreme Lord of the Earth and of the Sky that she remain where she is."

Then he orders his followers to make the necessary arrangements for the safe journey of their future king and his brother.

The children stand passive in their gay dress, but are bewildered and afraid.

mah phru has risen to her feet. She appears as if turned to bronze—a model of restraint and dignity, blent with colour and beauty and infinite grace.

THE CURTAIN DESCENDS SLOWLY

SCENE II

The same night.

The home of the Chinese Wizard, hip loong, by the river—a place fitted with Chinese things: Dragons of gold with eyes of jade gleaming from out dim corners, Buddhas of gigantic size fashioned of priceless metals with heads that move, swinging banners with fringes of many-coloured stones, lanterns with glass slides on which are painted grotesque figures. The air is full of the scent of joss sticks. The Wizard reclines on a divan, inhaling opium slowly, clothed with the subdued gorgeousness of China—blue and tomato-red predominate. He has the appearance of a wrinkled walnut. His forehead is a lattice-work of wrinkles. His pigtail, braided with red, is twisted round his head. His hands are as claws. The effect is weird, unearthly.

Enter mah phru.

The Wizard silently motions her to some piled-up cushions at a little distance. He listens to what she tells him. He appears unmoved, at a recital apparently full of tragedy. Only the eyes of the dragons move, and the heads of the Buddhas go slowly like pendulums. When she has finished speaking, hip loong makes reply.

"This is how passion always ends. I have lived for a thousand years; and on this planet it is ever the same."

mah phru is not listening.

"How can I go to my children?" she demands, once again.

"I can turn you into a bird," the Wizard says. "You can fly to the palace and walk and watch ever on that terrace in the rose gardens above the sea."

"What bird?" she asks, trembling.

"You shall have the form of the white paddy bird, because, though a woman and foolish as women ever are, you are very pure ivory. O! daughter of man and of love."

To this mah phru dissents. She paces the long room.

"Transform me into a peacock; they are more beautiful."

The Wizard, leaning on his elbow, smiles, and the smile is a revelation of a mocking comprehension.

"So be it." He bows his head.

The lights fade one by one.

CURTAIN

SCENE III

The Gardens of the Palace of the King.

Time: late afternoon.

Colonnades of roses stretch away on every side. Fountains play, throwing a shower on water-lilies of monstrous size. Peacocks walk with stately tread across the green turf. Only one, larger and more beautiful than the rest, is perched alone, with drooping head and folded tail, on the broad-pillared terrace that overhangs the sea. The scene is aglow with light and colour, yet holds a shadowed silence.

Enter some courtiers, who converse in perturbed fashion as they go towards the Palace.

Enter moung pho mhin and u. rai gyan thoo, accompanied by the

Court Physicians and Astrologers.

"The King cannot live beyond the night," the Physicians say. The sudden, mysterious illness that has attacked him defies their skill.

The Astrologers declare that the stars in their courses fight against his recovery; unless a miracle should happen, the new day will see him dead.

The Ministers regard each other in consternation; then walk the terrace with bent heads.

The peacock on the wall spreads its tail and utters a melancholy cry of poignant pain.

The listeners start in superstitious horror.

The peacock folds its tail and resumes its meditations.

"That bird is not as other birds," one astrologer declares. "I have watched it for years past—it is ever alone—the others all avoid it. I think it has a soul."

"You mistake," replies his colleague; "it is but an evil Nat. [32] Observe its eyes: they are not those of a bird; they are those of a spirit in prison."

They pass on in the wake of the ministers.

The peacock closes its eyes.

Enter the two young princes, accompanied by two great Pegu hounds. They converse in subdued tones, strolling slowly. They are followed by pages of honour, carrying grain, which the young men proceed to distribute amongst the birds as they rapidly approach them. The peacock on the wall never stirs; she watches the young men always. Then the elder one comes with a handful of food and proffers it, but the peacock does not eat.

"I shall never understand you, Queen of the Kingdom of Birds," he says, and strokes her feathers. At his touch the plumage scintillates with a brighter, a more exquisite sheen.

He murmurs to the bird in soft tones and mythical words. He tells it that the fear of everyone is that the King is mortally stricken, for he lies yonder in most strange and evil agony; that the hearts of himself and his brother are numb with the sorrow that knows no language. The bird listens eagerly. And if the King should go, he, the speaker, will reign in his stead. The prospect fills him with fear. He desires, as also his brother, if the King must die, to return to dwell in the forest with the mother who he knows awaits them there.

The peacock spreads its wings as if for flight, then crouches down once more, and over it watches the young prince.

The sun envelops them both in a sudden shaft of rose and purple and gold. A servant descends and comes across the grass. He shikoes profoundly to the two young men, lifting up his hands in the deepest reverence of Burmah.

"The Lord of the Earth and the Sky desires his sons; he nears the Great Unknown."

CURTAIN

SCENE IV

The retreat of hip loong, the Wizard.

Time: the same night.

The curtain discovers mah phru, who has returned to human form, and the Wizard together.

He tells her that he has restored her to her former state only because she has implored him to do so; that her life is measured by hours as a consequence of such insensate folly in breaking the vow of five years back.

"But the King will live," she murmurs.

"The King will live. He will find happiness with someone fairer than you. That is well. Your life for his. It is the price."

"The price is nothing. Have I not looked on my heart's beloved one for five years—looked on his face—heard his voice—trembled with joy at his footsteps? Have I not waited and watched? Have I not gazed on my sons and seen their royal bearing, and known their touch?"

26

"You are, then, content?"

"You are a Wizard—you can read that I am."

"It is not I that am a Wizard—it is Love. That is the only Wizard this world knows."

CURTAIN

SCENE V

The bed-chamber of the King—vast and shadowy. On heaped-up cushions and covers of yellow and blue, under a pearl-sewn creamy velvet baldaquin, embroidered with peacocks, lies meng beng, mortally stricken; his face bears the ashen pallor that only dark skins know. The ministers, the servants, the courtiers, the countless motley gathering of an Eastern Court are scattered in anxious groups, watching, waiting, murmuring. Only the space near the couch is clear. Without, the dawn breaks over the sea, and, stealing through the opening, makes the great chamber flush till it looks like porphyry.

The tolling of a deep gong and the voices of a myriad birds invade the throbbing silence of the Palace.

"He passes," murmur the physicians. Everyone's gaze turns to the dying man.

"Yet his star is in the ascendant," say the astrologers. The risen sun touches him with its light like a caress. He opens his eyes. His sons advance. They raise him high on his cushions and give a restorative. The end has come. Suddenly he rallies slightly.

The doors at the far end are rudely opened. A woman, young and lovely, advances, thrusting roughly aside the many hands stretched out to bar her path.

She reaches the King.

"I bring you life, Star of my Soul," she cries, "I bring you life," and so saying, falls dead at his feet.

The Courtiers rush forward.

The King rises.

He stands erect.

The sun lies like a golden benediction over all.

Jewels glitter.

The whole world of birds sing.

THE CURTAIN FALLS

Footnotes:

[4] One of the greatest feasts of the Buddhist year.

[6] Spire.

[32] Fairy.

IMPRESSIONS OF AMERICA

TO
WALTER LEDGER:
PIGNUS
AMICITIÆ.

IMPRESSIONS.

I.

LE JARDIN.

The lily's withered chalice falls

Around its rod of dusty gold,

And from the beech trees on the wold

The last wood-pigeon coos and calls.

The gaudy leonine sunflower

Hangs black and barren on its stalk,

And down the windy garden walk

The dead leaves scatter,—hour by hour.

Pale privet-petals white as milk

Are blown into a snowy mass;

The roses lie upon the grass,

Like little shreds of crimson silk.

II.

LA MER.

A white mist drifts across the shrouds,

A wild moon in this wintry sky

Gleams like an angry lion's eye

Out of a mane of tawny clouds.

The muffled steersman at the wheel

Is but a shadow in the gloom;—

And in the throbbing engine room

Leap the long rods of polished steel.

The shattered storm has left its trace

Upon this huge and heaving dome,

For the thin threads of yellow foam

Float on the waves like ravelled lace.

Oscar Wilde.

PREFACE.

Oscar Wilde visited America in the year 1882. Interest in the Æsthetic School, of which he was already the acknowledged master, had sometime previously spread to the United States, and it is said that the production of the Gilbert and Sullivan opera, "Patience,"[1] in which he and his disciples were held up to ridicule, determined him to pay a visit to the States to give some lectures explaining what he meant by Æstheticism, hoping thereby to interest, and possibly to instruct and elevate our transatlantic cousins.

He set sail on board the "Arizona" on Saturday, December 24th, 1881, arriving in New York early in the following year. On landing he was bombarded by journalists eager to interview the distinguished stranger. "Punch," in its issue of January 14th, in a happy vein, parodied these interviewers, the most amusing passage in which referred to "His Glorious Past," wherein Wilde was made to say, "Precisely—I took the Newdigate. Oh! no doubt, every year some man gets the Newdigate; but not every year does Newdigate get an Oscar."

At Omaha, where, under the auspices of the Social Art Club, Wilde delivered a lecture on "Decorative Art," he described his impressions of many American houses as being "illy designed, decorated shabbily, and in bad taste, filled with furniture that was not honestly made, and was out of character." This statement gave rise to the following verses:—

What a shame and what a pity,

In the streets of London City

Mr. Wilde is seen no more.

Far from Piccadilly banished,

He to Omaha has vanished.

Horrid place, which swells ignore.

On his back a coat he beareth,

Such as Sir John Bennet weareth,

Made of velvet—strange array!

Legs Apollo might have sighed for,

Or great Hercules have died for,

His knee breeches now display.

Waving sunflower and lily,

He calls all the houses "illy

Decorated and designed."

For of taste they've not a tittle;

They may chew and they may whittle;

But they're all born colour-blind!

His lectures dealt almost exclusively with the subjects of Art and Dress Reform. In the course of one lecture he remarked that the most impressive room he had yet entered in America was the one in Camden Town where he met Walt Whitman. It contained plenty of fresh air and sunlight. On the table was a simple cruse of water. This led to a parody, in the style of Whitman, describing an imaginary interview between the two poets, which appeared in "The Century" a few months later. Wilde is called Narcissus and Whitman Paumanokides.

Paumanokides:—

Who may this be?

This young man clad unusually with loose locks, languorous, glidingly toward me advancing,

Toward the ceiling of my chamber his orbic and expressive eyeballs uprolling,

38

and so on, to which Narcissus replies,

O clarion, from whose brazen throat,

Strange sounds across the seas are blown,

Where England, girt as with a moat,

A strong sea-lion sits alone!

Of the lectures which he delivered in America only one has been preserved, namely that on the English Renaissance. This was his first lecture, and it was delivered in New York on January 9th, 1882. According to a contemporary account in the "New York Herald" a distinguished and crowded audience assembled in Chickering Hall that evening to listen to one who "was well worth seeing, his short breeches and silk stockings showing to even better advantage upon the stage than in the gilded drawing-rooms, where the young   Apostle has heretofore been seen in New York."[2]

On leaving the States in the "fall" of the year Wilde proceeded to Canada and thence to Nova Scotia, arriving in Halifax in the second week of October. Of his visit there we have no record except an amusing interview described in a local paper a few days later. He was dressed in a velvet jacket with an ordinary linen collar and neck tie and he wore trousers. "Mr. Wilde," the interviewer states, "was communicative and genial; he said he found Canada pleasant, but in answer to a question as to whether European or American women were the more   beautiful, he dexterously evaded his querist."

As regards poetry he expressed his opinion that Poe was the greatest American poet, and that Walt Whitman, if not a poet, was a man who sounded a strong note, perhaps neither prose nor poetry, but something of his own that was "grand, original and unique."

During his tour in America Wilde "happened to find" himself (as he has himself described it), in Louisville, Kentucky. The subject he had selected to speak on was the Mission of Art in the Nineteenth Century. In the course of his lecture he had occasion to quote Keats' Sonnet on Blue "as an example of the poet's delicate sense of colour-harmonies." After the lecture there came round to see him "a lady of middle age, with a sweet gentle manner and most musical voice," who introduced herself as Mrs. Speed, the daughter of George Keats, and she invited the lecturer to come and examine the Keats manuscripts in her possession.

Some months afterwards when lecturing in California he received a letter from this lady asking him to accept the original manuscript of the sonnet which he had quoted.

Mention must be made of Wilde's first play, a drama in blank verse entitled "Vera, or the Nihilists." It had been arranged that, before his departure for America, this play should be performed at the Adelphi Theatre, London, with Mrs. Bernard Beere as the heroine, on Saturday, December 17th, 1881, but a few weeks before the date fixed for the first performance, the author decided to postpone the production "owing to the state of political feeling in England."

On his return to England in 1883 Wilde started on a lecturing tour, the first being to the Art Students of the Royal Academy at their Club in Golden Square on June 30th. Ten days later he spoke at Prince's Hall on his "Personal Impressions of America," and on subsequent occasions at Margate, Ramsgate and Southampton. On Monday, July 30th he lectured at Southport and on the following Thursday he went to Liverpool to welcome Mrs. Langtry on her return from America, and the same afternoon he left on his second visit to the States in order to superintend the rehearsals of "Vera," which it had been arranged to produce at the Union Square Theatre, New York, on August 20th following. The piece was not a success—it was, indeed, the only failure Wilde had. However, his next play, which he called his "Opus Secundum," also a blank verse tragedy, had a successful run in America in 1891. This was "The Duchess of Padua," played by Lawrence Barrett, under the title of "Guido Ferranti." This has not been seen in England, nor is it even possible for Wilde's admirers to read this early offspring of his pen, for only twenty copies were printed for acting purposes in America and of these but one is known to be in existence, in this country at least.

An authorised German translation was made by Max Meyerfeld and the first performance took place at the German Theatre in Hamburg about a year

40

ago. An English version is advertised from a piratical publisher in Paris but it is only a translation from the German back into English.

Towards the end of September 1883 Oscar Wilde returned to England and immediately began "an all round lecturing tour," his first visit being to Wandsworth Town Hall on Monday, September 24th, when he delivered to an enthusiastic audience a lecture on his "Impressions of America," which is contained in the following pages. He was dressed, a London paper of the time states, "in ordinary evening costume, and carried an orange-coloured silk handkerchief in his breast. He spoke with great fluency, in a voice now and then singularly musical, and only once or twice made a scarcely perceptible reference to notes." The lecture was under the auspices of a local Literary Society, and the principle residents of the district turned out "en masse." The Chairman, the Rev. John Park, in introducing the lecturer, said there were two reasons why he was glad to welcome him, and he thought his own feelings would be shared by the audience. They must all plead guilty to a feeling of curiosity, he hoped a laudable one, to see and hear Mr. Wilde for his own sake, and they were also glad to hear about America—a country which many might regard as a kind of Elysium.

On March 5th in the following year Wilde lectured at the Crystal Palace on his American experiences, and on April 26th he "preached his Gospel in the East-end," when it is recorded that his audience was not only delighted with his humour, but was "surprised at the excellent good sense he talked." His subject was a plea in favour of "art for schools," and many of his remarks about the English system of elementary education—with its insistence on "the population of places that no one ever wants to go to," and its "familiarity with the lives of persons who probably never existed"—were said to be quite worthy of Ruskin. A contemporary account adds that Wilde "showed himself a pupil of Mr. Ruskin's, too, in insisting on the importance of every child being taught some handicraft, and in looking forward to the time when a boy would rather look at a bird or even draw it than throw "his customary stone!"

The British "gamin" has not made much progress in this respect during the last twenty years!

His lectures on "Dress," with the newspaper correspondence which they evoked, including some of Oscar Wilde's replies in his most characteristic vein, must be reserved for a future volume.

STUART MASON.

Oxford, January 1906.

1. First produced at the Opera Comique, April 23rd, 1881. Wilde was burlesqued as Reginald Bunthorne, a Fleshly Poet.

2. Wilde repeated this lecture throughout the States during his tour. At Rochester, on February 7th, he met with a most disorderly reception on the part of the College Students. Two days later Mr. Joaquin Miller, of St. Louis, wrote to Wilde saying that he had "read with shame about the behaviour of those ruffians." To this Wilde replied, "I thank you for your chivalrous and courteous letter," and in the course of his letter makes a more special attack on that critic whom he terms "the itinerant libeller of New England."

IMPRESSIONS OF AMERICA.

I fear I cannot picture America as altogether an Elysium—perhaps, from the ordinary standpoint I know but little about the country. I cannot give its latitude or longitude; I cannot compute the value of its dry goods, and I have no very close acquaintance with its politics. These are matters which may not interest you, and they certainly are not interesting to me.

The first thing that struck me on landing in America was that if the Americans are not the most well-dressed people in the world, they are the most comfortably dressed. Men are seen there with the dreadful chimney-pot hat, but there are very few hatless men; men wear the shocking swallow-tail coat, but few are to be seen with no coat at all. There is an air of comfort in the appearance of the people which is a marked contrast to that seen in this country, where, too often, people are seen in close contact with rags.

The next thing particularly noticeable is that everybody seems in a hurry to catch a train. This is a state of things which is not favourable to poetry or romance. Had Romeo or Juliet been in a constant state of anxiety about trains, or had their minds been agitated by the question of return-tickets, Shakespeare could not have given us those lovely balcony scenes which are so full of poetry and pathos.

America is the noisiest country that ever existed. One is waked up in the morning, not by the singing of the nightingale, but by the steam whistle. It is surprising that the sound practical sense of the Americans does not reduce this intolerable noise. All Art depends upon exquisite and delicate sensibility, and such continual turmoil must ultimately be destructive of the musical faculty.

There is not so much beauty to be found in American cities as in Oxford, Cambridge, Salisbury or Winchester, where are lovely relics of a beautiful age; but still there is a good deal of beauty to be seen in them now and then, but only where the American has not attempted to create it. Where the Americans have attempted to produce beauty they have signally failed. A remarkable characteristic of the Americans is the manner in which they have applied science to modern life.

This is apparent in the most cursory stroll through New York. In England an inventor is regarded almost as a   crazy man, and in too many instances invention ends in disappointment and poverty. In America an inventor is honoured, help is forthcoming, and the exercise of ingenuity, the application of science to the work of man, is there the shortest road to wealth. There is no country in the world where machinery is so lovely as in America.

I have always wished to believe that the line of strength and the line of beauty are one. That wish was realised when I contemplated American machinery. It was not until I had seen the water-works at Chicago that I realised the wonders of machinery; the rise and fall of the steel rods, the symmetrical motion of the great wheels is the most beautifully rhythmic thing I have ever seen.[3]   One is impressed in America, but not favourably impressed, by the inordinate size of everything. The country seems to try to bully one into a belief in its power by its impressive bigness.

I was disappointed with Niagara—most people must be disappointed with Niagara. Every American bride is taken there, and the sight of the stupendous waterfall must be one of the earliest, if not the keenest, disappointments in American married life. One sees it under bad conditions, very far away, the point of view not showing the splendour of the water. To appreciate it really one has to see it from underneath the fall, and to do that it is necessary to be dressed in a yellow oil-skin, which is as ugly as a mackintosh—and I hope none of you ever wears one. It is a consolation to know, however, that such an artist as Madame Bernhardt has not only worn that yellow, ugly dress, but has been photographed in it.

Perhaps the most beautiful part of America is the West, to reach which, however, involves a journey by rail of six days, racing along tied to an ugly tin-kettle of a steam engine. I found but poor consolation for this journey in the fact that the boys who infest the cars and sell everything that one can eat—or should not eat—were selling editions of my poems vilely printed on a kind

44

of grey blotting paper, for the low price of ten cents.[4] Calling these boys on one side I told them that though poets like to be popular they desire to be paid, and selling editions of my poems without giving me a profit is dealing a blow at literature which must have a disastrous effect on poetical aspirants. The invariable reply that they made was that they themselves made a profit out of the transaction and that was all they cared about.

It is a popular superstition that in America a visitor is invariably addressed as "Stranger." I was never once addressed as "Stranger." When I went to Texas I was called "Captain"; when I got to the centre of the country I was addressed as "Colonel," and, on arriving at the borders of Mexico, as "General." On the whole, however, "Sir," the old English method of addressing people is the most common.

It is, perhaps, worth while to note that what many people call Americanisms are really old English expressions which have lingered in our colonies while they have been lost in our own country. Many people imagine that the term "I guess," which is so common in America, is purely an American expression, but it was used by John Locke in his work on "The Understanding," just as we now use "I think."[5]

It is in the colonies, and not in the mother country, that the old life of the country really exists. If one wants to realise what English Puritanism is— not at its worst (when it is very bad), but at its best, and then it is not very good—I do not think one can find much of it in England, but much can be found about Boston and Massachusetts. We have got rid of it. America still preserves it, to be, I hope, a short-lived curiosity.

San Francisco is a really beautiful city. China Town, peopled by Chinese labourers, is the most artistic town I have ever come across. The people— strange, melancholy Orientals, whom many people would call common, and they are certainly very poor—have determined that they will have nothing about them that is not beautiful. In the Chinese restaurant, where these navvies meet to have supper in the evening, I found them drinking tea out of china cups as delicate as the petals of a rose-leaf, whereas at the gaudy hotels I was supplied with a delf cup an inch and a half thick. When the Chinese bill was presented it was made out on rice paper, the account being done in Indian ink as fantastically as if an artist had been etching little birds on a fan.

Salt Lake City contains only two buildings of note, the chief being the Tabernacle, which is in the shape of a soup-kettle. It is decorated by the only native artist, and he has treated religious subjects in the naive spirit of the early Florentine painters, representing people of our own day in the dress of the period side by side with people of Biblical history who are clothed in some romantic costume.

The building next in importance is called the Amelia Palace, in honour of one of Brigham Young's wives. When he died the present president of the Mormons stood up in the Tabernacle and said that it had been revealed to him that he was to have the Amelia Palace, and that on this subject there were to be no more revelations of any kind!

From Salt Lake City one travels over the great plains of Colorado and up the Rocky Mountains, on the top of which is Leadville, the richest city in the world. It has also got the reputation of being the roughest, and every man carries a revolver. I was told that if I went there they would   be sure to shoot me or my travelling manager. I wrote and told them that nothing that they could do to my travelling manager would intimidate me. They are miners—men working in metals, so I lectured to them on the Ethics of Art. I read them passages from the autobiography of Benvenuto Cellini and they seemed much delighted. I was reproved by my hearers for not having brought him with me. I explained that he had been dead for some little time which elicited the enquiry "Who shot him"? They afterwards took me to a dancing saloon where I saw the only rational method of art criticism I have ever come across. Over the piano was printed a notice:—

PLEASE DO NOT SHOOT THE PIANIST.

HE IS DOING HIS BEST.

The mortality among pianists in that place is marvellous. Then they asked me to supper, and having accepted, I had to descend a mine in a rickety bucket in which it was impossible to be graceful. Having got into the heart of the mountain I had supper, the first course being whisky, the second whisky and the third whisky.

I went to the Theatre to lecture and I was informed that just before I went there two men had been seized for committing a murder, and in that theatre they had been brought on to the stage at eight o'clock in the evening, and then and there tried and executed before a crowded audience. But I found these miners very charming and not at all rough.

Among the more elderly inhabitants of the South I found a melancholy tendency to date every event of importance by the late war. "How beautiful the moon is to-night," I once remarked to a gentleman who was standing next to me. "Yes," was his reply, "but you should have seen it before the war."

So infinitesimal did I find the knowledge of Art, west of the Rocky Mountains, that an art patron—one who in his day had been a miner—actually sued the railroad company for damages because the plaster cast of Venus of Milo, which he had imported from Paris, had been delivered minus the arms. And, what is more surprising still, he gained his case and the damages.

Pennsylvania, with its rocky gorges and woodland scenery, reminded me of Switzerland. The prairie reminded me of a piece of blotting-paper.

The Spanish and French have left behind them memorials in the beauty of their names. All the cities that have beautiful names derive them from the Spanish or the French. The English people give intensely ugly names to places. One place had such an ugly name that I refused to lecture there. It was called Grigsville. Supposing I had founded a school of Art there—fancy "Early Grigsville." Imagine a School of Art teaching "Grigsville Renaissance."

As for slang I did not hear much of it, though a young lady who had changed her clothes after an afternoon dance did say that "after the heel kick she shifted her day goods."

American youths are pale and precocious, or sallow and supercilious, but

American girls are pretty and charming—little oases of pretty unreasonableness in a vast desert of practical common-sense.

Every American girl is entitled to have twelve young men devoted to her. They remain her slaves and she rules them with charming nonchalance.

The men are entirely given to business; they have, as they say, their brains in front of their heads. They are also exceedingly acceptive of new ideas. Their education is practical. We base the education of children entirely on books, but we must give a child a mind before we can instruct the mind. Children have a natural antipathy to books—handicraft should be the basis of education. Boys and girls should be taught to use their hands to make something, and they would be less apt to destroy and be mischievous.

In going to America one learns that poverty is not a necessary accompaniment to civilisation. There at any rate is a country that has no trappings, no pageants and no gorgeous ceremonies. I saw only two processions—one was the Fire Brigade preceded by the Police, the other was the Police preceded by the Fire Brigade.

Every man when he gets to the age of twenty-one is allowed a vote, and thereby immediately acquires his political education. The Americans are the best politically educated people in the world. It is well worth one's while to go to a country which can teach us the beauty of the word FREEDOM and the value of the thing LIBERTY.

3. In a poem published in an American magazine on February 15th, 1882, Wilde wrote

"And in the throbbing engine room

Leap the long rods of polished steel."

4. Poems by Oscar Wilde. Also his Lecture on the English Renaissance. The Seaside Library, Vol. lviii. No. 1183, January 19th, 1882. 4to. Pp. 32. New York: George Munro, Publisher.

A copy of this edition was sold by auction in New York last year for eight dollars.

5. See An Essay concerning Human Understanding, IV. xii. 10.

A still more striking instance of the use of this expression is to be found in the same writer's Thoughts concerning Education, s. 28, where he says:—"Once in four and twenty hours, I think, is enough; and nobody, I guess, will think it too much."

OSCAR WILDE IN AMERICA.

An interesting account of Oscar Wilde, at the time of his American tour, was given in the Lady's Pictorial a few weeks after his arrival in New York, the city which he described as "one huge Whiteley's shop."

His Abode.

He was interviewed in a room which was intensely warm and the sofa on which the poet reclined was drawn up to the fire. An immense wolf rug, bordered with scarlet, was thrown over it and half-encircled his graceful form in its warm embrace. Wilde was wearied. In a languid, half enervated manner he gently sipped hot chocolate from a cup by his side. Occasionally he inhaled a long, deep whiff from a smouldering cigarette held lightly in his white and shapely hand.

His Dress.

He was attired in a smoking suit of dark brown velvet faced with lapels of red quilted silk. The ends of a long dark necktie floated over the facing like sea-weed on foam tinged by the dying sun. Dark brown nether garments, striped with red up the seam, and patent leather shoes with light cloth uppers completed the rest of the poet's costume.

His favourite colour is said to have been something between brown and green, a tint "that never was on sea or sky," and he had a complete suit made of it. A white walking-stick which he was in the habit of carrying was presented to him at the Acropolis and was said to have been cut from the olive groves of the Academia. Only in the evening was he wont to don knee breeches, "but evening and morning alike," adds his interviewer, "find him neither more nor less than a man, and always a perfect gentleman."

His appearance.

Long masses of dark brown hair, parted in the middle, fell in odd curves of beauty over his broad shoulders. He wore neither beard nor moustache.

The full, rather sensuous lips, now pressed close together with momentary tension, now parted in kindly smile, showed to perfection the nobility of his countenance.

A Grecian nose and a well-tinged flush of health on the poet's face added all that was required to make it a truly remarkable one. The eyes were large, dark[6] and ever-changing in expression. He was a charming companion who could tell racy stories and repeat bons mots of those whom society delighted to honour, and at the same time could cap quotations from Greek authors.

6. A French writer, M. Joseph-Renaud, recently described Wilde's eyes as being blue, while Lord Alfred Douglas affirms that they were green.

About Author

Oscar Fingal O'Flahertie Wills Wilde (16 October 1854 – 30 November 1900) was an Irish poet and playwright. After writing in different forms throughout the 1880s, the early 1890s saw him become one of the most popular playwrights in London. He is best remembered for his epigrams and plays, his novel The Picture of Dorian Gray, and the circumstances of his criminal conviction for "gross indecency", imprisonment, and early death at age 46.

Wilde's parents were successful Anglo-Irish intellectuals in Dublin. A young Wilde learned to speak fluent French and German. At university, Wilde read Greats; he demonstrated himself to be an exceptional classicist, first at Trinity College Dublin, then at Oxford. He became associated with the emerging philosophy of aestheticism, led by two of his tutors, Walter Pater and John Ruskin. After university, Wilde moved to London into fashionable cultural and social circles.

As a spokesman for aestheticism, he tried his hand at various literary activities: he published a book of poems, lectured in the United States and Canada on the new "English Renaissance in Art" and interior decoration, and then returned to London where he worked prolifically as a journalist. Known for his biting wit, flamboyant dress and glittering conversational skill, Wilde became one of the best-known personalities of his day. At the turn of the 1890s, he refined his ideas about the supremacy of art in a series of dialogues and essays, and incorporated themes of decadence, duplicity, and beauty into what would be his only novel, The Picture of Dorian Gray (1890). The opportunity to construct aesthetic details precisely, and combine them with larger social themes, drew Wilde to write drama. He wrote Salome (1891) in French while in Paris but it was refused a licence for England due to an absolute prohibition on the portrayal of Biblical subjects on the English stage. Unperturbed, Wilde produced four society comedies in the early 1890s, which made him one of the most successful playwrights of late-Victorian London.

At the height of his fame and success, while The Importance of Being Earnest (1895) was still being performed in London, Wilde had the Marquess of Queensberry prosecuted for criminal libel. The Marquess was the father of Wilde's lover, Lord Alfred Douglas. The libel trial unearthed evidence that caused Wilde to drop his charges and led to his own arrest and trial for gross indecency with men. After two more trials he was convicted and sentenced to two years' hard labour, the maximum penalty, and was jailed from 1895 to 1897. During his last year in prison, he wrote De Profundis (published posthumously in 1905), a long letter which discusses his spiritual journey through his trials, forming a dark counterpoint to his earlier philosophy of pleasure. On his release, he left immediately for France, never to return to Ireland or Britain. There he wrote his last work, The Ballad of Reading Gaol (1898), a long poem commemorating the harsh rhythms of prison life.

Early life

Oscar Wilde was born at 21 Westland Row, Dublin (now home of the Oscar Wilde Centre, Trinity College), the second of three children born to Anglo-Irish Sir William Wilde and Jane Wilde, two years behind his brother William ("Willie"). Wilde's mother had distant Italian ancestry, and under the pseudonym "Speranza" (the Italian word for 'hope'), wrote poetry for the revolutionary Young Irelanders in 1848; she was a lifelong Irish nationalist. She read the Young Irelanders' poetry to Oscar and Willie, inculcating a love of these poets in her sons. Lady Wilde's interest in the neo-classical revival showed in the paintings and busts of ancient Greece and Rome in her home.

William Wilde was Ireland's leading oto-ophthalmologic (ear and eye) surgeon and was knighted in 1864 for his services as medical adviser and assistant commissioner to the censuses of Ireland. He also wrote books about Irish archaeology and peasant folklore. A renowned philanthropist, his dispensary for the care of the city's poor at the rear of Trinity College, Dublin, was the forerunner of the Dublin Eye and Ear Hospital, now located at Adelaide Road. On his father's side Wilde was descended from a Dutchman, Colonel de Wilde, who went to Ireland with King William of Orange's invading army in 1690, and numerous Anglo-Irish ancestors. On his mother's side, Wilde's ancestors included a bricklayer from County Durham, who emigrated to Ireland sometime in the 1770s.

Wilde was baptised as an infant in St. Mark's Church, Dublin, the local Church of Ireland (Anglican) church. When the church was closed, the records were moved to the nearby St. Ann's Church, Dawson Street. Davis Coakley mentions a second baptism by a Catholic priest, Father Prideaux Fox, who befriended Oscar's mother circa 1859. According to Fox's testimony in Donahoe's Magazine in 1905, Jane Wilde would visit his chapel in Glencree, County Wicklow, for Mass and would take her sons with her. She asked Father Fox in this period to baptise her sons.

Fox described it in this way:

"I am not sure if she ever became a Catholic herself but it was not long before she asked me to instruct two of her children, one of them being the future erratic genius, Oscar Wilde. After a few weeks I baptized these two children, Lady Wilde herself being present on the occasion.

In addition to his children with his wife, Sir William Wilde was the father of three children born out of wedlock before his marriage: Henry Wilson, born in 1838 to one woman, and Emily and Mary Wilde, born in 1847 and 1849, respectively, to a second woman. Sir William acknowledged paternity of his illegitimate or "natural" children and provided for their education, arranging for them to be reared by his relatives rather than with his legitimate children in his family household with his wife.

In 1855, the family moved to No. 1 Merrion Square, where Wilde's sister, Isola, was born in 1857. The Wildes' new home was larger. With both his parents' success and delight in social life, the house soon became the site of a "unique medical and cultural milieu". Guests at their salon included Sheridan Le Fanu, Charles Lever, George Petrie, Isaac Butt, William Rowan Hamilton and Samuel Ferguson.

Until he was nine, Oscar Wilde was educated at home, where a French nursemaid and a German governess taught him their languages. He attended Portora Royal School in Enniskillen, County Fermanagh, from 1864 to 1871. Until his early twenties, Wilde summered at the villa, Moytura House, which his father had built in Cong, County Mayo. There the young Wilde and his brother Willie played with George Moore.

Isola died at age nine of meningitis. Wilde's poem "Requiescat" is written to her memory.

"Tread lightly, she is near

Under the snow

Speak gently, she can hear

the daisies grow"

University education: 1870s

Trinity College, Dublin

Wilde left Portora with a royal scholarship to read classics at Trinity College, Dublin, from 1871 to 1874, sharing rooms with his older brother Willie Wilde. Trinity, one of the leading classical schools, placed him with scholars such as R. Y. Tyrell, Arthur Palmer, Edward Dowden and his tutor, Professor J. P. Mahaffy, who inspired his interest in Greek literature. As a student Wilde worked with Mahaffy on the latter's book Social Life in Greece. Wilde, despite later reservations, called Mahaffy "my first and best teacher" and "the scholar who showed me how to love Greek things".For his part, Mahaffy boasted of having created Wilde; later, he said Wilde was "the only blot on my tutorship".

The University Philosophical Society also provided an education, as members discussed intellectual and artistic subjects such as Dante Gabriel Rossetti and Algernon Charles Swinburne weekly. Wilde quickly became an established member – the members' suggestion book for 1874 contains two pages of banter (sportingly) mocking Wilde's emergent aestheticism. He presented a paper titled "Aesthetic Morality". At Trinity, Wilde established himself as an outstanding student: he came first in his class in his first year, won a scholarship by competitive examination in his second and, in his finals, won the Berkeley Gold Medal in Greek, the University's highest academic award. He was encouraged to compete for a demyship to Magdalen College, Oxford – which he won easily, having already studied Greek for over nine years.

Magdalen College, Oxford

At Magdalen, he read Greats from 1874 to 1878, and from there he applied to join the Oxford Union, but failed to be elected.

Attracted by its dress, secrecy, and ritual, Wilde petitioned the Apollo Masonic Lodge at Oxford, and was soon raised to the "Sublime Degree of Master Mason".During a resurgent interest in Freemasonry in his third year, he commented he "would be awfully sorry to give it up if I secede from the Protestant Heresy". Wilde's active involvement in Freemasonry lasted only for the time he spent at Oxford; he allowed his membership of the Apollo University Lodge to lapse after failing to pay subscriptions.

Catholicism deeply appealed to him, especially its rich liturgy, and he discussed converting to it with clergy several times. In 1877, Wilde was left speechless after an audience with Pope Pius IX in Rome.He eagerly read the books of Cardinal Newman, a noted Anglican priest who had converted to Catholicism and risen in the church hierarchy. He became more serious in 1878, when he met the Reverend Sebastian Bowden, a priest in the Brompton Oratory who had received some high-profile converts. Neither his father, who threatened to cut off his funds, nor Mahaffy thought much of the plan; but mostly Wilde, the supreme individualist, balked at the last minute from pledging himself to any formal creed. On the appointed day of his baptism, Wilde sent Father Bowden a bunch of altar lilies instead. Wilde did retain a lifelong interest in Catholic theology and liturgy.

While at Magdalen College, Wilde became particularly well known for his role in the aesthetic and decadent movements. He wore his hair long, openly scorned "manly" sports though he occasionally boxed, and he decorated his rooms with peacock feathers, lilies, sunflowers, blue china and other objets d'art. He once remarked to friends, whom he entertained lavishly, "I find it harder and harder every day to live up to my blue china." The line quickly became famous, accepted as a slogan by aesthetes but used against them by critics who sensed in it a terrible vacuousness. Some elements disdained the aesthetes, but their languishing attitudes and showy costumes became a recognised pose. Wilde was once physically attacked by a group of four fellow students, and dealt with them single-handedly, surprising critics. By his third year Wilde had truly begun to develop himself and his myth, and considered his learning to be more expansive than what was within the prescribed texts. This attitude resulted in his being rusticated for one term, after he had returned late to a college term from a trip to Greece with Mahaffy.

Wilde did not meet Walter Pater until his third year, but had been enthralled by his Studies in the History of the Renaissance, published during Wilde's final year in Trinity. Pater argued that man's sensibility to beauty should be refined above all else, and that each moment should be felt to its fullest extent. Years later, in De Profundis, Wilde described Pater's Studies... as "that book that has had such a strange influence over my life". He learned tracts of the book by heart, and carried it with him on travels in later years. Pater gave Wilde his sense of almost flippant devotion to art, though he gained a purpose for it through the lectures and writings of critic John Ruskin. Ruskin despaired at the self-validating aestheticism of Pater, arguing that the importance of art lies in its potential for the betterment of society. Ruskin admired beauty, but believed it must be allied with, and applied to, moral good. When Wilde eagerly attended Ruskin's lecture series The Aesthetic and Mathematic Schools of Art in Florence, he learned about aesthetics as the non-mathematical elements of painting. Despite being given to neither early rising nor manual labour, Wilde volunteered for Ruskin's project to convert a swampy country lane into a smart road neatly edged with flowers.

Wilde won the 1878 Newdigate Prize for his poem "Ravenna", which reflected on his visit there the year before, and he duly read it at Encaenia. In November 1878, he graduated with a double first in his B.A. of Classical Moderations and Literae Humaniores (Greats). Wilde wrote to a friend, "The dons are 'astonied' beyond words – the Bad Boy doing so well in the end!"

Apprenticeship of an aesthete: 1880s

Debut in society

After graduation from Oxford, Wilde returned to Dublin, where he met again Florence Balcombe, a childhood sweetheart. She became engaged to Bram Stoker and they married in 1878. Wilde was disappointed but stoic:

he wrote to her, remembering "the two sweet years – the sweetest years of all my youth" during which they had been close. He also stated his intention to "return to England, probably for good." This he did in 1878, only briefly visiting Ireland twice after that.

Unsure of his next step, Wilde wrote to various acquaintances enquiring about Classics positions at Oxford or Cambridge. The Rise of Historical Criticism was his submission for the Chancellor's Essay prize of 1879, which, though no longer a student, he was still eligible to enter. Its subject, "Historical Criticism among the Ancients" seemed ready-made for Wilde – with both his skill in composition and ancient learning – but he struggled to find his voice with the long, flat, scholarly style. Unusually, no prize was awarded that year.

With the last of his inheritance from the sale of his father's houses, he set himself up as a bachelor in London. The 1881 British Census listed Wilde as a boarder at 1 (now 44) Tite Street, Chelsea, where Frank Miles, a society painter, was the head of the household. Wilde spent the next six years in London and Paris, and in the United States, where he travelled to deliver lectures.

He had been publishing lyrics and poems in magazines since entering Trinity College, especially in Kottabos and the Dublin University Magazine. In mid-1881, at 27 years old, he published Poems, which collected, revised and expanded his poems.

The book was generally well received, and sold out its first print run of 750 copies. Punch was less enthusiastic, saying "The poet is Wilde, but his poetry's tame". By a tight vote, the Oxford Union condemned the book for alleged plagiarism. The librarian, who had requested the book for the library, returned the presentation copy to Wilde with a note of apology. Biographer Richard Ellmann argues that Wilde's poem "Hélas!" was a sincere, though flamboyant, attempt to explain the dichotomies the poet saw in himself; one line reads: "To drift with every passion till my soul

Is a stringed lute on which all winds can play".

The book had further printings in 1882. It was bound in a rich, enamel parchment cover (embossed with gilt blossom) and printed on hand-made Dutch paper; over the next few years, Wilde presented many copies to the dignitaries and writers who received him during his lecture tours.

America: 1882

Aestheticism was sufficiently in vogue to be caricatured by Gilbert and Sullivan in Patience (1881). Richard D'Oyly Carte, an English impresario, invited Wilde to make a lecture tour of North America, simultaneously priming the pump for the US tour of Patience and selling this most charming aesthete to the American public. Wilde journeyed on the SS Arizona, arriving 2 January 1882, and disembarking the following day. Originally planned to last four months, it continued for almost a year due to the commercial success. Wilde sought to transpose the beauty he saw in art into daily life. This was a practical as well as philosophical project: in Oxford he had surrounded himself with blue china and lilies, and now one of his lectures was on interior design.

When asked to explain reports that he had paraded down Piccadilly in London carrying a lily, long hair flowing, Wilde replied, "It's not whether I did it or not that's important, but whether people believed I did it". Wilde believed that the artist should hold forth higher ideals, and that pleasure and beauty would replace utilitarian ethics.

Wilde and aestheticism were both mercilessly caricatured and criticised in the press; the Springfield Republican, for instance, commented on Wilde's behaviour during his visit to Boston to lecture on aestheticism, suggesting that Wilde's conduct was more a bid for notoriety rather than devotion to beauty and the aesthetic. T. W. Higginson, a cleric and abolitionist, wrote in "Unmanly Manhood" of his general concern that Wilde, "whose only distinction is that he has written a thin volume of very mediocre verse", would improperly influence the behaviour of men and women.

According to biographer Michèle Mendelssohn, Wilde was the subject of anti-Irish caricature and was portrayed as a monkey, a blackface performer and a Christy's Minstrel throughout his career. "Harper's Weekly put a sunflower-worshipping monkey dressed as Wilde on the front of the January 1882 issue. The magazine didn't let its reputation for quality impede its expression of what are now considered odious ethnic and racial ideologies. The drawing stimulated other American maligners and, in England, had a full-page reprint in the Lady's Pictorial. ... When the National Republican discussed Wilde, it was to explain 'a few items as to the animal's pedigree.' And on 22 January 1882 the Washington Post illustrated the Wild Man of Borneo alongside Oscar Wilde of England and asked 'How far is it from this to this?' "Though his press reception was hostile, Wilde was well received in diverse settings across America; he drank whiskey with miners in Leadville, Colorado, and was fêted at the most fashionable salons in many cities he visited.

London life and marriage

His earnings, plus expected income from The Duchess of Padua, allowed him to move to Paris between February and mid-May 1883. While there he met Robert Sherard, whom he entertained constantly. "We are dining on the Duchess tonight", Wilde would declare before taking him to an expensive restaurant. In August he briefly returned to New York for the production of Vera, his first play, after it was turned down in London. He reportedly entertained the other passengers with "Ave Imperatrix!, A Poem on England", about the rise and fall of empires. E. C. Stedman, in Victorian Poets, describes this "lyric to England" as "manly verse – a poetic and eloquent invocation". The play was initially well received by the audience, but when the critics wrote lukewarm reviews, attendance fell sharply and the play closed a week after it had opened.

Wilde had to return to England, where he continued to lecture on topics including Personal Impressions of America, The Value of Art in Modern Life, and Dress.

In London, he had been introduced in 1881 to Constance Lloyd, daughter of Horace Lloyd, a wealthy Queen's Counsel, and his wife. She happened to be visiting Dublin in 1884, when Wilde was lecturing at the Gaiety Theatre. He proposed to her, and they married on 29 May 1884 at the Anglican St James's Church, Paddington, in London. Although Constance had an annual allowance of £250, which was generous for a young woman (equivalent to about £25,600 in current value), the Wildes had relatively luxurious tastes. They had preached to others for so long on the subject of design that people expected their home to set new standards. No. 16, Tite Street was duly renovated in seven months at considerable expense. The couple had two sons together, Cyril (1885) and Vyvyan (1886). Wilde became the sole literary signatory of George Bernard Shaw's petition for a pardon of the anarchists arrested (and later executed) after the Haymarket massacre in Chicago in 1886.

Robert Ross had read Wilde's poems before they met at Oxford in 1886. He seemed unrestrained by the Victorian prohibition against homosexuality, and became estranged from his family. By Richard Ellmann's account, he was a precocious seventeen-year-old who "so young and yet so knowing, was determined to seduce Wilde". According to Daniel Mendelsohn, Wilde, who had long alluded to Greek love, was "initiated into homosexual sex" by Ross, while his "marriage had begun to unravel after his wife's second pregnancy, which left him physically repelled".

Prose writing: 1886–91

Journalism and editorship: 1886–89

Criticism over artistic matters in The Pall Mall Gazette provoked a letter in self-defence, and soon Wilde was a contributor to that and other journals during 1885–87. He enjoyed reviewing and journalism; the form suited his style. He could organise and share his views on art, literature and life, yet in a format less tedious than lecturing. Buoyed up, his reviews were largely chatty and positive. Wilde, like his parents before him, also supported the cause of Irish nationalism. When Charles Stewart Parnell was falsely accused of inciting murder, Wilde wrote a series of astute columns defending him in the Daily Chronicle.

His flair, having previously been put mainly into socialising, suited journalism and rapidly attracted notice. With his youth nearly over, and a family to support, in mid-1887 Wilde became the editor of The Lady's World magazine, his name prominently appearing on the cover. He promptly renamed it as The Woman's World and raised its tone, adding serious articles on parenting, culture, and politics, while keeping discussions of fashion and arts. Two pieces of fiction were usually included, one to be read to children, the other for the ladies themselves. Wilde worked hard to solicit good contributions from his wide artistic acquaintance, including those of Lady Wilde and his wife Constance, while his own "Literary and Other Notes" were themselves popular and amusing.

The initial vigour and excitement which he brought to the job began to fade as administration, commuting and office life became tedious. At the same time as Wilde's interest flagged, the publishers became concerned anew about circulation: sales, at the relatively high price of one shilling, remained low. Increasingly sending instructions to the magazine by letter, Wilde began a new period of creative work and his own column appeared less regularly.In October 1889, Wilde had finally found his voice in prose and, at the end of the second volume, Wilde left The Woman's World. The magazine outlasted him by one issue.

If Wilde's period at the helm of the magazine was a mixed success from an organizational point of view, it played a pivotal role in his development as a writer and facilitated his ascent to fame. Whilst Wilde the journalist supplied articles under the guidance of his editors, Wilde the editor was forced to learn to manipulate the literary marketplace on his own terms.

During the late 1880s, Wilde was a close friend of the artist James NcNeill Whistler and they dined together on many occasions. At one of these dinners, Whistler said a bon mot that Wilde found particularly witty, Wilde exclaimed that he wished that he had said it, and Whistler retorted "You will, Oscar, you will".Herbert Vivian—a mutual friend of Wilde and Whistler—attended the dinner and recorded it in his article The Reminiscences of a Short Life which appeared in The Sun in 1889. The article alleged that Wilde had a habit of passing off other people's witticisms as his own—especially Whistler's. Wilde considered Vivian's article to be a scurrilous betrayal, and it directly caused the broken friendship between Wilde and Whistler. The Reminiscences also caused great acrimony between Wilde and Vivian, Wilde accusing Vivian of "the inaccuracy of an eavesdropper with the method of a blackmailer" and banishing Vivian from his circle.

Shorter fiction

Wilde published The Happy Prince and Other Tales in 1888, and had been regularly writing fairy stories for magazines. In 1891 he published two more collections, Lord Arthur Savile's Crime and Other Stories, and in September A House of Pomegranates was dedicated "To Constance Mary Wilde". "The Portrait of Mr. W. H.", which Wilde had begun in 1887, was first published in Blackwood's Edinburgh Magazine in July 1889.It is a short story, which reports a conversation, in which the theory that Shakespeare's sonnets were written out of the poet's love of the boy actor "Willie Hughes", is advanced, retracted, and then propounded again. The only evidence for this is two supposed puns within the sonnets themselves.

The anonymous narrator is at first sceptical, then believing, finally flirtatious with the reader: he concludes that "there is really a great deal to be said of the Willie Hughes theory of Shakespeare's sonnets." By the end fact and fiction have melded together.Arthur Ransome wrote that Wilde "read something of himself into Shakespeare's sonnets" and became fascinated with the "Willie Hughes theory" despite the lack of biographical evidence for the historical William Hughes' existence. Instead of writing a short but serious essay on the question, Wilde tossed the theory amongst the three characters of the story, allowing it to unfold as background to the plot. The story thus is an early masterpiece of Wilde's combining many elements that interested him: conversation, literature and the idea that to shed oneself of an idea one must first convince another of its truth.Ransome concludes that Wilde succeeds precisely because the literary criticism is unveiled with such a deft touch.

Though containing nothing but "special pleading", it would not, he says "be possible to build an airier castle in Spain than this of the imaginary William Hughes" we continue listening nonetheless to be charmed by the telling. "You must believe in Willie Hughes," Wilde told an acquaintance, "I almost do, myself."

Essays and dialogues

Wilde, having tired of journalism, had been busy setting out his aesthetic ideas more fully in a series of longer prose pieces which were published in the major literary-intellectual journals of the day. In January 1889, The Decay of Lying: A Dialogue appeared in The Nineteenth Century, and Pen, Pencil and Poison, a satirical biography of Thomas Griffiths Wainewright, in The Fortnightly Review, edited by Wilde's friend Frank Harris. Two of Wilde's four writings on aesthetics are dialogues: though Wilde had evolved professionally from lecturer to writer, he retained an oral tradition of sorts. Having always excelled as a wit and raconteur, he often composed by assembling phrases, bons mots and witticisms into a longer, cohesive work.

Wilde was concerned about the effect of moralising on art; he believed in art's redemptive, developmental powers: "Art is individualism, and individualism is a disturbing and disintegrating force. There lies its immense value. For what it seeks is to disturb monotony of type, slavery of custom, tyranny of habit, and the reduction of man to the level of a machine." In his only political text, The Soul of Man Under Socialism, he argued political conditions should establish this primacy – private property should be abolished, and cooperation should be substituted for competition. At the same time, he stressed that the government most amenable to artists was no government at all. Wilde envisioned a society where mechanisation has freed human effort from the burden of necessity, effort which can instead be expended on artistic creation. George Orwell summarised, "In effect, the world will be populated by artists, each striving after perfection in the way that seems best to him."

This point of view did not align him with the Fabians, intellectual socialists who advocated using state apparatus to change social conditions, nor did it endear him to the monied classes whom he had previously entertained. Hesketh Pearson, introducing a collection of Wilde's essays in 1950, remarked how The Soul of Man Under Socialism had been an inspirational text for revolutionaries in Tsarist Russia but laments that in the Stalinist era "it is doubtful whether there are any uninspected places in which it could now be hidden".

Wilde considered including this pamphlet and The Portrait of Mr. W.H., his essay-story on Shakespeare's sonnets, in a new anthology in 1891, but eventually decided to limit it to purely aesthetic subjects. Intentions packaged revisions of four essays: The Decay of Lying, Pen, Pencil and Poison, The Truth of Masks (first published 1885), and The Critic as Artist in two parts. For Pearson the biographer, the essays and dialogues exhibit every aspect of Wilde's genius and character: wit, romancer, talker, lecturer, humanist and scholar and concludes that "no other productions of his have as varied an appeal". 1891 turned out to be Wilde's annus mirabilis; apart from his three collections he also produced his only novel.

The Picture of Dorian Gray

The first version of The Picture of Dorian Gray was published as the lead story in the July 1890 edition of Lippincott's Monthly Magazine, along with five others. The story begins with a man painting a picture of Gray. When Gray, who has a "face like ivory and rose leaves", sees his finished portrait, he breaks down. Distraught that his beauty will fade while the portrait stays beautiful, he inadvertently makes a Faustian bargain in which only the painted image grows old while he stays beautiful and young. For Wilde, the purpose of art would be to guide life as if beauty alone were its object. As Gray's portrait allows him to escape the corporeal ravages of his hedonism, Wilde sought to juxtapose the beauty he saw in art with daily life.

Reviewers immediately criticised the novel's decadence and homosexual allusions; The Daily Chronicle for example, called it "unclean", "poisonous", and "heavy with the mephitic odours of moral and spiritual putrefaction". Which he clarified his stance on ethics and aesthetics in art – "If a work of art is rich and vital and complete, those who have artistic instincts will see its beauty and those to whom ethics appeal more strongly will see its moral lesson." He nevertheless revised it extensively for book publication in 1891: six new chapters were added, some overtly decadent passages and homo-eroticism excised, and a preface was included consisting of twenty two epigrams, such as "Books are well written, or badly written. That is all."

Contemporary reviewers and modern critics have postulated numerous possible sources of the story, a search Jershua McCormack argues is futile because Wilde "has tapped a root of Western folklore so deep and ubiquitous that the story has escaped its origins and returned to the oral tradition." Wilde claimed the plot was "an idea that is as old as the history of literature but to which I have given a new form".Modern critic Robin McKie considered the novel to be technically mediocre, saying that the conceit of the plot had guaranteed its fame, but the device is never pushed to its full.On the other hand, Robert McCrum of The Guardian deemed it the 27th best novel ever written in English, calling it "an arresting, and slightly camp, exercise in late-Victorian gothic."

Theatrical career: 1892–95

Salomé

The 1891 census records the Wildes' residence at 16 Tite Street, where he lived with his wife Constance and two sons. Wilde though, not content with being better known than ever in London, returned to Paris in October 1891, this time as a respected writer. He was received at the salons littéraires, including the famous mardis of Stéphane Mallarmé, a renowned symbolist poet of the time. Wilde's two plays during the 1880s, Vera; or, The Nihilists and The Duchess of Padua, had not met with much success. He had continued his interest in the theatre and now, after finding his voice in prose, his thoughts turned again to the dramatic form as the biblical iconography of Salome filled his mind. One evening, after discussing depictions of Salome throughout history, he returned to his hotel and noticed a blank copybook lying on the desk, and it occurred to him to write in it what he had been saying. The result was a new play, Salomé, written rapidly and in French.

A tragedy, it tells the story of Salome, the stepdaughter of the tetrarch Herod Antipas, who, to her stepfather's dismay but mother's delight, requests the head of Jokanaan (John the Baptist) on a silver platter as a reward for dancing the Dance of the Seven Veils. When Wilde returned to London just before Christmas the Paris Echo referred to him as "le great event" of the season. Rehearsals of the play, starring Sarah Bernhardt, began but the play was refused a licence by the Lord Chamberlain, since it depicted biblical characters. Salome was published jointly in Paris and London in 1893, but was not performed until 1896 in Paris, during Wilde's later incarceration.

Comedies of society

Wilde, who had first set out to irritate Victorian society with his dress and talking points, then outrage it with Dorian Gray, his novel of vice hidden beneath art, finally found a way to critique society on its own terms. Lady Windermere's Fan was first performed on 20 February 1892 at St James's Theatre, packed with the cream of society. On the surface a witty comedy, there is subtle subversion underneath: "it concludes with collusive concealment rather than collective disclosure". The audience, like Lady Windermere, are forced to soften harsh social codes in favour of a more nuanced view. The play was enormously popular, touring the country for months, but largely trashed by conservative critics. It was followed by A Woman of No Importance in 1893, another Victorian comedy, revolving around the spectre of illegitimate births, mistaken identities and late revelations.Wilde was commissioned to write two more plays and An Ideal Husband, written in 1894,followed in January 1895.

Peter Raby said these essentially English plays were well-pitched, "Wilde, with one eye on the dramatic genius of Ibsen, and the other on the commercial competition in London's West End, targeted his audience with adroit precision".

Queensberry family

In mid-1891 Lionel Johnson introduced Wilde to Lord Alfred Douglas, Johnson's cousin and an undergraduate at Oxford at the time.Known to his family and friends as "Bosie", he was a handsome and spoilt young man. An intimate friendship sprang up between Wilde and Douglas and by 1893 Wilde was infatuated with Douglas and they consorted together regularly in a tempestuous affair. If Wilde was relatively indiscreet, even flamboyant, in the way he acted, Douglas was reckless in public. Wilde, who was earning up to £100 a week from his plays (his salary at The Woman's World had been £6), indulged Douglas's every whim: material, artistic or sexual.

Douglas soon initiated Wilde into the Victorian underground of gay prostitution and Wilde was introduced to a series of young working-class male prostitutes from 1892 onwards by Alfred Taylor. These infrequent rendezvous usually took the same form: Wilde would meet the boy, offer him gifts, dine him privately and then take him to a hotel room. Unlike Wilde's idealised relations with Ross, John Gray, and Douglas, all of whom remained part of his aesthetic circle, these consorts were uneducated and knew nothing of literature. Soon his public and private lives had become sharply divided; in De Profundis he wrote to Douglas that "It was like feasting with panthers; the danger was half the excitement... I did not know that when they were to strike at me it was to be at another's piping and at another's pay."

Douglas and some Oxford friends founded a journal, The Chameleon, to which Wilde "sent a page of paradoxes originally destined for the Saturday Review". "Phrases and Philosophies for the Use of the Young" was to come under attack six months later at Wilde's trial, where he was forced to defend the magazine to which he had sent his work.In any case, it became unique: The Chameleon was not published again.

Lord Alfred's father, the Marquess of Queensberry, was known for his outspoken atheism, brutish manner and creation of the modern rules of boxing. Queensberry, who feuded regularly with his son, confronted Wilde and Lord Alfred about the nature of their relationship several times, but Wilde was able to mollify him. In June 1894, he called on Wilde at 16 Tite Street, without an appointment, and clarified his stance: "I do not say that you are it, but you look it, and pose at it, which is just as bad. And if I catch you and my son again in any public restaurant I will thrash you" to which Wilde responded: "I don't know what the Queensberry rules are, but the Oscar Wilde rule is to shoot on sight".His account in De Profundis was less triumphant: "It was when, in my library at Tite Street, waving his small hands in the air in epileptic fury, your father... stood uttering every foul word his foul mind could think of, and screaming the loathsome threats he afterwards with such cunning carried out". Queensberry only described the scene once, saying Wilde had "shown him the white feather", meaning he had acted in a cowardly way. Though trying to remain calm, Wilde saw that he was becoming ensnared in a brutal family quarrel. He did not wish to bear Queensberry's insults, but he knew to confront him could lead to disaster were his liaisons disclosed publicly.

The Importance of Being Earnest

Wilde's final play again returns to the theme of switched identities: the play's two protagonists engage in "bunburying" (the maintenance of alternative personas in the town and country) which allows them to escape Victorian social mores.Earnest is even lighter in tone than Wilde's earlier comedies. While their characters often rise to serious themes in moments of crisis, Earnest lacks the by-now stock Wildean characters: there is no "woman with a past", the principals are neither villainous nor cunning, simply idle cultivés, and the idealistic young women are not that innocent. Mostly set in drawing rooms and almost completely lacking in action or violence, Earnest lacks the self-conscious decadence found in The Picture of Dorian Gray and Salome.

The play, now considered Wilde's masterpiece, was rapidly written in Wilde's artistic maturity in late 1894. It was first performed on 14 February 1895, at St James's Theatre in London, Wilde's second collaboration with George Alexander, the actor-manager. Both author and producer assiduously revised, prepared and rehearsed every line, scene and setting in the months before the premiere, creating a carefully constructed representation of late-Victorian society, yet simultaneously mocking it. During rehearsal Alexander requested that Wilde shorten the play from four acts to three, which the author did. Premieres at St James's seemed like "brilliant parties", and the opening of The Importance of Being Earnest was no exception. Allan Aynesworth (who played Algernon) recalled to Hesketh Pearson, "In my fifty-three years of acting, I never remember a greater triumph than [that] first night."Earnest's immediate reception as Wilde's best work to date finally crystallised his fame into a solid artistic reputation. The Importance of Being Earnest remains his most popular play.

Wilde's professional success was mirrored by an escalation in his feud with Queensberry. Queensberry had planned to insult Wilde publicly by throwing a bouquet of rotting vegetables onto the stage; Wilde was tipped off and had Queensberry barred from entering the theatre.Fifteen weeks later Wilde was in prison.

Trials

70

Wilde v. Queensberry

On 18 February 1895, the Marquess left his calling card at Wilde's club, the Albemarle, inscribed: "For Oscar Wilde, posing somdomite" Wilde, encouraged by Douglas and against the advice of his friends, initiated a private prosecution against Queensberry for libel, since the note amounted to a public accusation that Wilde had committed the crime of sodomy.

Queensberry was arrested for criminal libel; a charge carrying a possible sentence of up to two years in prison. Under the 1843 Libel Act, Queensberry could avoid conviction for libel only by demonstrating that his accusation was in fact true, and furthermore that there was some "public benefit" to having made the accusation openly. Queensberry's lawyers thus hired private detectives to find evidence of Wilde's homosexual liaisons.

Wilde's friends had advised him against the prosecution at a Saturday Review meeting at the Café Royal on 24 March 1895; Frank Harris warned him that "they are going to prove sodomy against you" and advised him to flee to France. Wilde and Douglas walked out in a huff, Wilde saying "it is at such moments as these that one sees who are one's true friends". The scene was witnessed by George Bernard Shaw who recalled it to Arthur Ransome a day or so before Ransome's trial for libelling Douglas in 1913. To Ransome it confirmed what he had said in his 1912 book on Wilde; that Douglas's rivalry for Wilde with Robbie Ross and his arguments with his father had resulted in Wilde's public disaster; as Wilde wrote in De Profundis. Douglas lost his case. Shaw included an account of the argument between Harris, Douglas and Wilde in the preface to his play The Dark Lady of the Sonnets.

The libel trial became a cause célèbre as salacious details of Wilde's private life with Taylor and Douglas began to appear in the press. A team of private detectives had directed Queensberry's lawyers, led by Edward Carson QC, to the world of the Victorian underground. Wilde's association with blackmailers and male prostitutes, cross-dressers and homosexual brothels was recorded, and various persons involved were interviewed, some being coerced to appear as witnesses since they too were accomplices to the crimes of which Wilde was accused.

The trial opened on 3 April 1895 before Justice Richard Henn Collins amid scenes of near hysteria both in the press and the public galleries. The extent of the evidence massed against Wilde forced him to declare meekly, "I am the prosecutor in this case"Wilde's lawyer, Sir Edward George Clarke, opened the case by pre-emptively asking Wilde about two suggestive letters Wilde had written to Douglas, which the defence had in its possession. He characterised the first as a "prose sonnet" and admitted that the "poetical language" might seem strange to the court but claimed its intent was innocent. Wilde stated that the letters had been obtained by blackmailers who had attempted to extort money from him, but he had refused, suggesting they should take the £60 (equal to £6,800 today) offered, "unusual for a prose piece of that length". He claimed to regard the letters as works of art rather than something of which to be ashamed.

Carson, a fellow Dubliner who had attended Trinity College, Dublin at the same time as Wilde, cross-examined Wilde on how he perceived the moral content of his works. Wilde replied with characteristic wit and flippancy, claiming that works of art are not capable of being moral or immoral but only well or poorly made, and that only "brutes and illiterates", whose views on art "are incalculably stupid", would make such judgements about art. Carson, a leading barrister, diverged from the normal practice of asking closed questions. Carson pressed Wilde on each topic from every angle, squeezing out nuances of meaning from Wilde's answers, removing them from their aesthetic context and portraying Wilde as evasive and decadent. While Wilde won the most laughs from the court, Carson scored the most legal points. To undermine Wilde's credibility, and to justify Queensberry's description of Wilde as a "posing somdomite", Carson drew from the witness an admission of his capacity for "posing", by demonstrating that he had lied about his age on oath. Playing on this, he returned to the topic throughout his cross-examination. Carson also tried to justify Queensberry's characterisation by quoting from Wilde's novel, The Picture of Dorian Gray, referring in particular to a scene in the second chapter, in which Lord Henry Wotton explains his decadent philosophy to Dorian, an "innocent young man", in Carson's words.

Carson then moved to the factual evidence and questioned Wilde about his friendships with younger, lower-class men. Wilde admitted being on a first-name basis and lavishing gifts upon them, but insisted that nothing untoward had occurred and that the men were merely good friends of his. Carson repeatedly pointed out the unusual nature of these relationships and insinuated that the men were prostitutes. Wilde replied that he did not believe in social barriers, and simply enjoyed the society of young men. Then Carson asked Wilde directly whether he had ever kissed a certain servant boy, Wilde responded, "Oh, dear no. He was a particularly plain boy – unfortunately ugly – I pitied him for it." Carson pressed him on the answer, repeatedly asking why the boy's ugliness was relevant. Wilde hesitated, then for the first time became flustered: "You sting me and insult me and try to unnerve me; and at times one says things flippantly when one ought to speak more seriously."

In his opening speech for the defence, Carson announced that he had located several male prostitutes who were to testify that they had had sex with Wilde. On the advice of his lawyers, Wilde dropped the prosecution. Queensberry was found not guilty, as the court declared that his accusation that Wilde was "posing as a Somdomite" was justified, "true in substance and in fact".Under the Libel Act 1843, Queensberry's acquittal rendered Wilde legally liable for the considerable expenses Queensberry had incurred in his defence, which left Wilde bankrupt.

Regina v. Wilde

After Wilde left the court, a warrant for his arrest was applied for on charges of sodomy and gross indecency. Robbie Ross found Wilde at the Cadogan Hotel, Pont Street, Knightsbridge, with Reginald Turner; both men advised Wilde to go at once to Dover and try to get a boat to France; his mother advised him to stay and fight. Wilde, lapsing into inaction, could only say, "The train has gone. It's too late."On 6 April 1895, Wilde was arrested for "gross indecency" under Section 11 of the Criminal Law Amendment Act 1885, a term meaning homosexual acts not amounting to buggery (an offence under a separate statute). At Wilde's instruction, Ross and Wilde's butler forced their way into the bedroom and library of 16 Tite Street, packing some personal effects, manuscripts, and letters. Wilde was then imprisoned on remand at Holloway, where he received daily visits from Douglas.

Events moved quickly and his prosecution opened on 26 April 1895, before Mr Justice Charles. Wilde pleaded not guilty. He had already begged Douglas to leave London for Paris, but Douglas complained bitterly, even wanting to give evidence; he was pressed to go and soon fled to the Hotel du Monde. Fearing persecution, Ross and many others also left the United Kingdom during this time. Under cross examination Wilde was at first hesitant, then spoke eloquently:

> **Charles Gill** (prosecuting): What is "the love that dare not speak its name"?

> **Wilde:** "The love that dare not speak its name" in this century is such a great affection of an elder for a younger man as there was between David and Jonathan, such as Plato made the very basis of his philosophy, and such as you find in the sonnets of Michelangelo and Shakespeare. It is that deep spiritual affection that is as pure as it is perfect. It dictates and pervades great works of art, like those of Shakespeare and Michelangelo, and those two letters of mine, such as they are. It is in this century misunderstood, so much misunderstood that it may be described as "the love that dare not speak its name", and on that account of it I am placed where I am now. It is beautiful, it is fine, it is the noblest form of affection. There is nothing unnatural about it. It is intellectual, and it repeatedly exists between an older and a younger man, when the older man has intellect, and the younger man has all the joy, hope and glamour of life before him. That it should be so, the world does not understand. The world mocks at it, and sometimes puts one in the pillory for it.

This response was counter-productive in a legal sense as it only served to reinforce the charges of homosexual behaviour.

The trial ended with the jury unable to reach a verdict. Wilde's counsel, Sir Edward Clarke, was finally able to get a magistrate to allow Wilde and his friends to post bail. The Reverend Stewart Headlam put up most of the £5,000 surety required by the court, having disagreed with Wilde's treatment by the press and the courts. Wilde was freed from Holloway and, shunning attention, went into hiding at the house of Ernest and Ada Leverson, two of his firm friends. Edward Carson approached Frank Lockwood QC, the Solicitor General and asked "Can we not let up on the fellow now?" Lockwood answered that he would like to do so, but feared that the case had become too politicised to be dropped.

The final trial was presided over by Mr Justice Wills. On 25 May 1895 Wilde and Alfred Taylor were convicted of gross indecency and sentenced to two years' hard labour. The judge described the sentence, the maximum allowed, as "totally inadequate for a case such as this", and that the case was "the worst case I have ever tried". Wilde's response "And I? May I say nothing, my Lord?" was drowned out in cries of "Shame" in the courtroom.

Imprisonment

When first I was put into prison some people advised me to try and forget who I was. It was ruinous advice. It is only by realising what I am that I have found comfort of any kind. Now I am advised by others to try on my release to forget that I have ever been in a prison at all. I know that would be equally fatal. It would mean that I would always be haunted by an intolerable sense of disgrace, and that those things that are meant for me as much as for anybody else – the beauty of the sun and moon, the pageant of the seasons, the music of daybreak and the silence of great nights, the rain falling through the leaves, or the dew creeping over the grass and making it silver – would all be tainted for me, and lose their healing power, and their power of communicating joy. To regret one's own experiences is to arrest one's own development. To deny one's own experiences is to put a lie into the lips of one's own life. It is no less than a denial of the soul.

De Profundis

Wilde was incarcerated from 25 May 1895 to 18 May 1897.

He first entered Newgate Prison in London for processing, then was moved to Pentonville Prison, where the "hard labour" to which he had been sentenced consisted of many hours of walking a treadmill and picking oakum (separating the fibres in scraps of old navy ropes), and where prisoners were allowed to read only the Bible and The Pilgrim's Progress.

A few months later he was moved to Wandsworth Prison in London. Inmates there also followed the regimen of "hard labour, hard fare and a hard bed", which wore harshly on Wilde's delicate health. In November he collapsed during chapel from illness and hunger. His right ear drum was ruptured in the fall, an injury that later contributed to his death. He spent two months in the infirmary.

Richard B. Haldane, the Liberal MP and reformer, visited Wilde and had him transferred in November to Reading Gaol, 30 miles (48 km) west of London on 23 November 1895. The transfer itself was the lowest point of his incarceration, as a crowd jeered and spat at him on the railway platform. He spent the remainder of his sentence there, addressed and identified only as "C33" – the occupant of the third cell on the third floor of C ward.

About five months after Wilde arrived at Reading Gaol, Charles Thomas Wooldridge, a trooper in the Royal Horse Guards, was brought to Reading to await his trial for murdering his wife on 29 March 1896; on 17 June Wooldridge was sentenced to death and returned to Reading for his execution, which took place on Tuesday, 7 July 1896 – the first hanging at Reading in 18 years. From Wooldridge's hanging, Wilde later wrote The Ballad of Reading Gaol.

Wilde was not, at first, even allowed paper and pen but Haldane eventually succeeded in allowing access to books and writing materials. Wilde requested, among others: the Bible in French; Italian and German grammars; some Ancient Greek texts, Dante's Divine Comedy, Joris-Karl Huysmans's new French novel about Christian redemption En route, and essays by St Augustine, Cardinal Newman and Walter Pater.

Between January and March 1897 Wilde wrote a 50,000-word letter to Douglas. He was not allowed to send it, but was permitted to take it with him when released from prison. In reflective mode, Wilde coldly examines his career to date, how he had been a colourful agent provocateur in Victorian society, his art, like his paradoxes, seeking to subvert as well as sparkle. His own estimation of himself was: one who "stood in symbolic relations to the art and culture of my age". It was from these heights that his life with Douglas began, and Wilde examines that particularly closely, repudiating him for what Wilde finally sees as his arrogance and vanity: he had not forgotten Douglas' remark, when he was ill, "When you are not on your pedestal you are not interesting." Wilde blamed himself, though, for the ethical degradation of character that he allowed Douglas to bring about in him and took responsibility for his own fall, "I am here for having tried to put your father in prison." The first half concludes with Wilde forgiving Douglas, for his own sake as much as Douglas's. The second half of the letter traces Wilde's spiritual journey of redemption and fulfilment through his prison reading. He realised that his ordeal had filled his soul with the fruit of experience, however bitter it tasted at the time.

> ... I wanted to eat of the fruit of all the trees in the garden of the world ... And so, indeed, I went out, and so I lived. My only mistake was that I confined myself so exclusively to the trees of what seemed to me the sun-lit side of the garden, and shunned the other side for its shadow and its gloom.

Wilde was released from prison on 19 May 1897 and sailed that evening for Dieppe, France. He never returned to the UK.

On his release, he gave the manuscript to Ross, who may or may not have carried out Wilde's instructions to send a copy to Douglas (who later denied having received it). The letter was partially published in 1905 as De Profundis; its complete and correct publication first occurred in 1962 in The Letters of Oscar Wilde.

Decline: 1897–1900

Exile

Though Wilde's health had suffered greatly from the harshness and diet of prison, he had a feeling of spiritual renewal. He immediately wrote to the Society of Jesus requesting a six-month Catholic retreat; when the request was denied, Wilde wept. "I intend to be received into the Catholic Church before long", Wilde told a journalist who asked about his religious intentions.

He spent his last three years impoverished and in exile. He took the name "Sebastian Melmoth", after Saint Sebastian and the titular character of Melmoth the Wanderer (a Gothic novel by Charles Maturin, Wilde's great-uncle).Wilde wrote two long letters to the editor of the Daily Chronicle, describing the brutal conditions of English prisons and advocating penal reform. His discussion of the dismissal of Warder Martin for giving biscuits to an anaemic child prisoner repeated the themes of the corruption and degeneration of punishment that he had earlier outlined in The Soul of Man under Socialism.

Wilde spent mid-1897 with Robert Ross in the seaside village of Berneval-le-Grand in northern France, where he wrote The Ballad of Reading Gaol, narrating the execution of Charles Thomas Wooldridge, who murdered his wife in a rage at her infidelity. It moves from an objective story-telling to symbolic identification with the prisoners. No attempt is made to assess the justice of the laws which convicted them but rather the poem highlights the brutalisation of the punishment that all convicts share. Wilde juxtaposes the executed man and himself with the line "Yet each man kills the thing he loves". He adopted the proletarian ballad form and the author was credited as "C33", Wilde's cell number in Reading Gaol. He suggested that it be published in Reynolds' Magazine, "because it circulates widely among the criminal classes – to which I now belong – for once I will be read by my peers – a new experience for me". It was an immediate roaring commercial success, going through seven editions in less than two years, only after which "[Oscar" was added to the title page, though many in literary circles had known Wilde to be the author. It brought him a small amount of money.

Although Douglas had been the cause of his misfortunes, he and Wilde were reunited in August 1897 at Rouen. This meeting was disapproved of by the friends and families of both men. Constance Wilde was already refusing to meet Wilde or allow him to see their sons, though she sent him money – three pounds a week. During the latter part of 1897, Wilde and Douglas lived together near Naples for a few months until they were separated by their families under the threat of cutting off all funds.

Wilde's final address was at the dingy Hôtel d'Alsace (now known as L'Hôtel), on rue des Beaux-Arts in Saint-Germain-des-Prés, Paris. "This poverty really breaks one's heart: it is so sale , so utterly depressing, so hopeless. Pray do what you can" he wrote to his publisher. He corrected and published An Ideal Husband and The Importance of Being Earnest, the proofs of which, according to Ellmann, show a man "very much in command of himself and of the play" but he refused to write anything else: "I can write, but have lost the joy of writing".

He wandered the boulevards alone and spent what little money he had on alcohol. A series of embarrassing chance encounters with hostile English visitors, or Frenchmen he had known in better days, drowned his spirit. Soon Wilde was sufficiently confined to his hotel to joke, on one of his final trips outside, "My wallpaper and I are fighting a duel to the death. One of us has got to go". On 12 October 1900 he sent a telegram to Ross: "Terribly weak. Please come". His moods fluctuated; Max Beerbohm relates how their mutual friend Reginald 'Reggie' Turner had found Wilde very depressed after a nightmare. "I dreamt that I had died, and was supping with the dead!" "I am sure", Turner replied, "that you must have been the life and soul of the party." Turner was one of the few of the old circle who remained with Wilde to the end and was at his bedside when he died.

Death

By 25 November 1900 Wilde had developed meningitis, then called "cerebral meningitis". Robbie Ross arrived on 29 November, sent for a priest, and Wilde was conditionally baptised into the Catholic Church by Fr Cuthbert Dunne, a Passionist priest from Dublin, Wilde having been baptised in the Church of Ireland and having moreover a recollection of Catholic baptism as a child, a fact later attested to by the minister of the sacrament, Fr Lawrence Fox. Fr Dunne recorded the baptism,

> As the voiture rolled through the dark streets that wintry night, the sad story of Oscar Wilde was in part repeated to me... Robert Ross knelt by the bedside, assisting me as best he could while I administered conditional baptism, and afterwards answering the responses while I

gave Extreme Unction to the prostrate man and recited the prayers for the dying. As the man was in a semi-comatose condition, I did not venture to administer the Holy Viaticum; still I must add that he could be roused and was roused from this state in my presence. When roused, he gave signs of being inwardly conscious... Indeed I was fully satisfied that he understood me when told that I was about to receive him into the Catholic Church and gave him the Last Sacraments... And when I repeated close to his ear the Holy Names, the Acts of Contrition, Faith, Hope and Charity, with acts of humble resignation to the Will of God, he tried all through to say the words after me.

Wilde died of meningitis on 30 November 1900. Different opinions are given as to the cause of the disease: Richard Ellmann claimed it was syphilitic; Merlin Holland, Wilde's grandson, thought this to be a misconception, noting that Wilde's meningitis followed a surgical intervention, perhaps a mastoidectomy; Wilde's physicians, Dr Paul Cleiss and A'Court Tucker, reported that the condition stemmed from an old suppuration of the right ear (from the prison injury, see above) treated for several years (une ancienne suppuration de l'oreille droite d'ailleurs en traitement depuis plusieurs années) and made no allusion to syphilis.

Burial

Wilde was initially buried in the Cimetière de Bagneux outside Paris; in 1909 his remains were disinterred and transferred to Père Lachaise Cemetery, inside the city. His tomb there was designed by Sir Jacob Epstein. It was commissioned by Robert Ross, who asked for a small compartment to be made for his own ashes, which were duly transferred in 1950. The modernist angel depicted as a relief on the tomb was originally complete with male genitalia, which were initially censored by French Authorities with a golden leaf. The genitals have since been vandalised; their current whereabouts are unknown. In 2000, Leon Johnson, a multimedia artist, installed a silver prosthesis to replace them. In 2011, the tomb was cleaned of the many lipstick marks left there by admirers and a glass barrier was installed to prevent further marks or damage.

The epitaph is a verse from The Ballad of Reading Gaol,

> And alien tears will fill for him
>
> Pity's long-broken urn,
>
> For his mourners will be outcast men,
>
> And outcasts always mourn.

Posthumous pardon

In 2017, Wilde was among an estimated 50,000 men who were pardoned for homosexual acts that were no longer considered offences under the Policing and Crime Act 2017. The Act is known informally as the Alan Turing law.

Honours

In 2014 Wilde was one of the inaugural honorees in the Rainbow Honor Walk, a walk of fame in San Francisco's Castro neighbourhood noting LGBTQ people who have "made significant contributions in their fields."

Biographies

Wilde's life has been the subject of numerous biographies since his death. The earliest were memoirs by those who knew him: often they are personal or impressionistic accounts which can be good character sketches, but are sometimes factually unreliable. Frank Harris, his friend and editor, wrote a biography, Oscar Wilde: His Life and Confessions (1916); though prone to exaggeration and sometimes factually inaccurate, it offers a good literary portrait of Wilde. Lord Alfred Douglas wrote two books about his relationship with Wilde. Oscar Wilde and Myself (1914), largely ghost-written by T. W. H. Crosland, vindictively reacted to Douglas's discovery that De Profundis was addressed to him and defensively tried to distance him from Wilde's scandalous reputation. Both authors later regretted their work. Later, in Oscar Wilde: A Summing Up (1939) and his Autobiography he was more sympathetic to Wilde. Of Wilde's other close friends, Robert Sherard; Robert Ross, his literary executor; and Charles Ricketts variously published biographies, reminiscences or correspondence. The first more or less objective biography of Wilde came about when Hesketh Pearson wrote Oscar Wilde: His Life and Wit (1946). In 1954 Wilde's son Vyvyan Holland published his memoir Son of Oscar Wilde, which recounts the difficulties Wilde's wife and children faced after his imprisonment. It was revised and updated by Merlin Holland in 1989.

Oscar Wilde, a critical study by Arthur Ransome was published in 1912. The book only briefly mentioned Wilde's life, but subsequently Ransome (and The Times Book Club) were sued for libel by Lord Alfred Douglas. In April 1913 Douglas lost the libel action after a reading of De Profundis refuted his claims.

Richard Ellmann wrote his 1987 biography Oscar Wilde, for which he posthumously won a National (USA) Book Critics Circle Award in 1988and a Pulitzer Prize in 1989. The book was the basis for the 1997 film Wilde, directed by Brian Gilbert and starring Stephen Fry as the title character.

Neil McKenna's 2003 biography, The Secret Life of Oscar Wilde, offers an exploration of Wilde's sexuality. Often speculative in nature, it was widely criticised for its pure conjecture and lack of scholarly rigour. Thomas Wright's Oscar's Books (2008) explores Wilde's reading from his childhood in Dublin to his death in Paris. After tracking down many books that once belonged to Wilde's Tite Street library (dispersed at the time of his trials), Wright was the first to examine Wilde's marginalia.

> Later on, I think everyone will recognise his achievements; his plays and essays will endure. Of course, you may think with others that his personality and conversation were far more wonderful than anything he wrote, so that his written works give only a pale reflection of his power. Perhaps that is so, and of course, it will be impossible to reproduce what is gone forever.

Robert Ross, 23 December 1900

In 2018, Matthew Sturgis' "Oscar: A Life," was published in London. The book incorporates rediscovered letters and other documents and is the most extensively researched biography of Wilde to appear since 1988.

Parisian literati, also produced several biographies and monographs on him. André Gide wrote In Memoriam, Oscar Wilde and Wilde also features in his journals. Thomas Louis, who had earlier translated books on Wilde into French, produced his own L'esprit d'Oscar Wilde in 1920. Modern books include Philippe Jullian's Oscar Wilde, and L'affaire Oscar Wilde, ou, Du danger de laisser la justice mettre le nez dans nos draps (The Oscar Wilde Affair, or, On the Danger of Allowing Justice to put its Nose in our Sheets) by Odon Vallet, a French religious historian. (Source: Wikipedia)

NOTABLE WORKS

The Picture of Dorian Gray (1890/1891). The first version of "The Picture of Dorian Gray" was published, in a form highly edited by the magazine, as the lead story in the July 1890 edition of Lippincott's Monthly Magazine. Wilde published the longer and revised version in book form in 1891, with an added preface.

Stories

"The Portrait of Mr. W. H." (1889)

The Happy Prince and Other Tales (1888, a collection of fairy tales) consisting of:

- "The Happy Prince"
- "The Nightingale and the Rose"
- "The Selfish Giant"
- "The Devoted Friend"
- "The Remarkable Rocket"

A House of Pomegranates (1891, fairy tales)

Lord Arthur Savile's Crime and Other Stories (1891) Including "The Canterville Ghost" first published in periodical form in 1887.

Complete Short Fiction. Penguin Classics, 2003. Edited with an Introduction and Notes by Ian Small. Contains all works listed above plus Poems in Prose (1894) and one very short 'Elder-tree' (fragment).

POEMS

Ravenna (1878) Winner of the Newdigate Prize.

Poems (1881) Wilde's collection of poetry and first publication.

The Sphinx (1894)

Poems in Prose (1894)

The Ballad of Reading Gaol (1898)

PLAYS

Vera; or, The Nihilists (1880)

The Duchess of Padua (1883)

Lady Windermere's Fan (1892)

A Woman of No Importance (1893)

Salomé (French version) (1893, first performed in Paris 1896)

Salomé: A Tragedy in One Act: Translated from the French of Oscar Wilde by Lord Alfred Douglas, illustrated by Aubrey Beardsley (1894)

An Ideal Husband (1895) (text)

The Importance of Being Earnest (1895) (text)

La Sainte Courtisane and A Florentine Tragedy Fragmentary. First published 1908 in Methuen's Collected Works

(Dates are dates of first performance, which approximate better to the probable date of composition than dates of publication.)

The Importance of Being Earnest and Other Plays. Penguin Classics, 2000. Edited with an Introduction, Commentaries and Notes by Richard Allen Cave. Contains all from above save the first two. Salome is in English.

As an appendix there is one excised scene from The Importance of Being Earnest.

POSTHUMOUS (PREVIOUSLY UNPUBLISHED)

De Profundis (Written 1895-97, in Reading Gaol). Expurgated edition published 1905; suppressed portions 1913, expanded version in The Letters of Oscar Wilde (1962).

The Rise of Historical Criticism (Written while at college) First published in 1905 (Sherwood Press, Hartford, CT) privately printed. Reprinted in Miscellanies, the last volume of the First Collected Edition (1908).

The First Collected Edition (Methuen & Co., 14 volumes) appeared in 1908 and contained many previously unpublished works.

The Second Collected Edition (Methuen & Co., 12 volumes) appeared in installments between 1909–11 and contained several other unpublished works.

The Letters of Oscar Wilde (Written 1868-1900) Published in 1962. Republished as The Complete Letters of Oscar Wilde (2000), with letters discovered since 1962, and new annotations by Merlin Holland.

The Women of Homer (Written 1876, while at college). First published in Oscar Wilde: The Women of Homer (2008) by The Oscar Wilde Society.

The Philosophy of Dress First published in The New-York Tribune (1885), published for the first time in book form in Oscar Wilde On Dress (2013).

MISATTRIBUTED

Teleny, or The Reverse of the Medal (Paris, 1893) has been attributed to Wilde, but its authorship is unclear. One theory is that it was a combined effort by several of Wilde's friends, which he may have edited.

Constance On September 14, 2011, Wilde's grandson Merlin Holland contested Wilde's claimed authorship of this play entitled Constance, scheduled to open that week in the King's Head Theatre. It was not, in fact, "Oscar Wilde's final play," as its producers were claiming. Holland said Wilde did sketch out the play's scenario in 1894, but "never wrote a word" of it, and that "it is dishonest to foist this on the public." The Artistic Director Adam Spreadbury-Maher of the King's Head Theatre and producer of Constance pointed out that Wilde's son, Vyvyan Holland, wrote in 1954, "a significant amount of the dialogue (of Constance) bears the authentic stamp of my father's hand". There is further proof that the developed scenario that Constance was reconstituted from was written by Wilde between 1897 and his death in 1900, rather than the 1894 George Alexander scenario which Merlin Holland quotes.

CPSIA information can be obtained
at www.ICGtesting.com
Printed in the USA
LVHW091020180820
663425LV00016BB/511